ABOUT THE BOOK

Set on Long Beach Island in the 1870's, this is the story of an eventful year in Jane Sibylla Jones' life.

Jane's father was the lighthouse keeper on the lonely, windswept island. Jane loved the island. She would have liked to run free on the beach and listen to the surf, sketch the birds and the unusual shells she found. But her mother believed that a girl of almost thirteen should learn to cook and sew and behave decorously. Mother missed the friends and shops she had left behind in Philadelphia, and she wanted to teach her only daughter all that a proper young lady should know.

Many things happened in the course of a year to affect Jane's feelings about herself and others. She formed a demanding friendship, witnessed a tragic shipwreck, and made a difficult decision about a promise.

This fresh, readable story by the author of *The Terrible Wave* is illustrated with drawings by Judith Gwyn Brown, which capture all the charm of the period setting. Jane is a warm, delightful girl with problems and worries as real as any girl's today.

SHADOW OF THE LIGHTHOUSE

by Marden Dahlstedt

drawings by Judith Gwyn Brown

COWARD, McCANN & GEOGHEGAN, INC.

NEW YORK

SBN: GB-698-30543-4
SBN: TR-698-20291-0
Library of Congress Catalog Card Number: 73-88537

PRINTED IN THE UNITED STATES OF AMERICA

08212

For
Richard Douglas Irwin III
and
Robert Whitney Irwin
growing up on the island a hundred years later

PART ONE

March - April
1870

❧ Chapter One ❧

"Jane Sibylla Jones!"

The tone of her mother's voice was a reprimand in itself as she stood frowning in the parlor doorway.

Jane looked up from the sketch pad that lay on her lap, and then down at the basket of rag balls at her feet.

"It's always the same"—the storm warnings were rising in her mother's tone—"no matter what job you're given, you always *do* just what pleases *you!*"

"I'm sorry, Mama," Jane began, her face flushing.

"Don't give me any excuses. I don't want to hear them. John Lippencott has hurt his foot, and your father has to take first watch, so I want to have supper early. Now, you just bundle up and go out and find T. J. I don't know what's gotten into that boy these days—he's never around when you want him."

Her mother turned and was gone with an angry swish of starched apron.

Jane glanced up to the mantel shelf where the huge conch shell lay gleaming and softly pearled pale pink and delicate amber. She examined the sketch she was making, and then with a deft movement she darkened the shading where the little tail of the shell curved around.

She could hear Mama banging pans in the kitchen.

Hurriedly Jane closed her sketchbook and tucked it on the bottom shelf of the bookstand next to the big Doré edition of *Paradise Lost*. She pulled the basket of rag balls, which she should have been sewing for rugs, back away from the crackling fire on the hearth, and went into the hall to get her coat.

As she stepped onto the wide porch a nor'east wind caught her long muffler and sent it streaming like a flag. Directly in front of her the dune grass, yellow now and sere, flowed like a river of gold. Beyond it, over the dune itself, she could hear the throbbing roar of the Atlantic surf.

Jane looked across the sandy yard to the tall red and white shaft of the lighthouse. Several sea gulls were riding the air currents near the top of the light where the narrow walkway circled, but she could see no black speck up there which might be her brother.

T. J. was up to something. Jane knew that, but she wasn't sure what it was. For the past several weeks he'd been acting in a most mysterious manner. Twice, during the day, she'd seen him standing on the cat-walk of the lighthouse, staring out to sea. Since he was forbidden to go up there this was highly unusual. And

while she hated to agree, her mother was right—he was always off by himself somewhere.

Jane circled the big, rambling, frame building that housed the two families of the lighthouse keepers, and struck off south along the beach. She was heading for the cedar grove about a half-mile down the island where T. J. had built his shanty. Occasionally she shouted his name, but the wind caught her voice and thinned it to wisps.

Actually Jane didn't mind this errand at all. In fact, she was delighted to be out of the house. Even though she had been living on the island for five years now, she still found it a place of continual enchantment. She had been seven when Papa took ill and had to give up his professorship at the University. She could remember only dimly the tall, narrow, red-brick house in Philadelphia, the clanging horse-drawn trolley cars and the bustle of shops. She felt that Long Beach Island, four miles out in the Atlantic Ocean off the New Jersey coast, was truly her home, here beneath the tall shadow of the Barnegat Light.

Suddenly she began to run. There was something about the beach that always made her want to fling her arms wide and shout. Maybe it was this great, wonderful feeling of space—the immense Atlantic on one side, the rolling dunes on the other, and empty beach stretching ahead—all wide-arching sky and wind. Her feet thudded on the hard-packed sand.

Jane was out of breath and tingling when she reached the clump of cedar trees. They were very old, small and wind-gnarled to fantastic shapes, like a troop of gnomes huddled on the beach. As she approached she could hear Sam barking, and in a minute a shaggy, shapeless ball of black fur came hurtling down the beach toward her across the sand.

Well, she thought, I was right. T. J.'s here.

Sam was like T. J.'s shadow. The dog even slept in his bed, to Mama's vast irritation.

"Hey, T. J.," she called. "Where are you? We're having supper early."

There was no sound but the *skritch-scratch* of a tree bough scraping in the wind. Ducking her head low, Jane pushed through the lower branches.

"Come on now—I know you're here," she complained.

The shanty was a crazy pile of salt-silvered boards nailed against the tallest tree, a venerable old fellow that reared its top high above the scrubby grove. Jane pushed open the rickety door.

The shanty was empty.

She stepped back outside, puzzled. Sam was still running around in a big circle, barking. Now she was becoming alarmed.

"T. J.—don't be funny," she called. "We don't have time for games! Mama's angry, and—"

She felt rather than heard the rustle above her head. Looking up she saw her little brother clinging to the top of the tree. It rocked with his slight weight as he began to climb down.

"Of all the dumb things," she began, as he edged his way nearer the ground. "What were you doing up there?"

T. J. slid the final few feet down the trunk of the tree and stood before her, brushing off his jacket. His smoky eyes, so like her own, regarded her calmly from beneath a long fringe of blond hair.

"Nothing," he replied serenely, "Come on, let's go home."

Exasperated, Jane swatted him on the arm.

"You make me so mad," she cried, remembering her fear. "Why didn't you answer when I called?"

T. J. had started for the beach without a backward glance.

"Oh, Jane," he said in a bored voice, "don't be so anachronistic!"

"Anachronistic" was T. J.'s new word. Just now, everything good, bad or indifferent, was "anachronistic." He would latch onto a new, unknown word joyfully, and use it with wild abandon for several months. A while back he had discovered "constipated" while reading a newspaper advertisement, and had happily described everything as being "nice and constipated," until Mama had taken him aside firmly and explained the word's meaning. Now it was "anachronistic."

Jane, puffing to keep up with him, followed along the windy beach. In the westering sun their two long blue shadows raced before them.

"Boy, talk about anachronistic!"—she had looked up the word in Papa's big dictionary—"you're the one who's anachronistic, sitting up in a tree in March!"

T. J. maintained a dignified silence.

Jane knew better than to badger him, for she had the same stubborn streak herself. But she was getting more and more curious. What was going on?

⊷Chapter Two⊶

Coming in out of the wind, the kitchen felt marvelous to Jane. The windows were shimmering with steam from kettles fragrantly murmuring on the stove, and the kerosene lamps glowed in warm pools of light. Papa and William were washing their hands at the wooden sink board.

Jane noticed T. J. sidle over, touch William's sleeve and shake his head briefly.

"Come now, don't dawdle," Mama said briskly. "We're late enough as it is."

They sat down in their accustomed places and bowed their heads. Pap's rich voice, with its hint of Welsh lilt, flowed quietly through the grace.

> For food and health and happy days
> Accept our gratitude and praise.

In serving others, Lord, may we
Return the blessings come from Thee.

Mama ladled a thick, steaming fish chowder from
the great blue Canton china tureen. There were biscuits, smoking hot and running with butter, and the
sweet-tart beach-plum jam that Jane had helped to
preserve last summer.

"John's foot looks badly swollen," Papa remarked.
"I think he may have broken a bone."

"Well, if Dr. DiGiovanni comes over to the island
tomorrow, I hope he brings some tonic with him.
These children look peaked."

Jane and T. J. exchanged wry glances. Last spring
they'd had to take a whole bottle of the dreadful stuff,
called Tonispah. It tasted like old socks smelled.

"Maybe Mr. Lippencott just sprained it," Jane remarked hopefully, "and then the doctor won't have to
come."

They loved the handsome young doctor from the
mainland, but they hated his medicines.

Papa smiled indulgently at Jane.

"I have some news for you," he said to her. "You
may be having a new friend tomorrow."

Before Jane could speak, Mama interrupted sharply.

"I'm not so sure about that, Will. I won't refuse to
teach the child, but she's not the sort I want as a friend
for Jane."

"Now Martha," her husband said mildly. "You don't
even know the girl. You can't judge sight unseen."

"Well, I know Rob Speers and any of his family
can't be much!"

Papa looked at Jane, who had been trying in vain to follow their conversation.

"I met old Rob Speers from Harvey Cedars down at the dock today. He asked if your mother will give lessons to his granddaughter, Dolly. He'll bring her up here in the morning."

There was no formal school on the island because there were too few children. Jane's mother had been a teacher before her marriage, and so she gave daily lessons to her own family and to the four Lippencott children who lived in the other half of the huge house. One room of the Jones' side was furnished as a schoolroom. Mrs. Jones was very strict, and every day from eight until noon they labored over their books and slates.

Jane was delighted at Papa's news. It would be fun to have a new face in their midst, for she plain purely detested Betsy and Clara Lippencott. She preferred being alone to being in their company. Betsy was a terrible tease, with a real mean streak thrown in, and the young Clara was getting to be just like her. Clara drove T. J. nearly to distraction with her tattling.

"What's she like, Papa?" Jane asked eagerly.

"I don't really know," he replied, helping himself to another bowl of chowder. "I've never seen her. She's fifteen, and has never had much formal schooling, though she can read and write, I gather."

"Well, that's a wonder," Mama said. "They live in such squalor. That old man shouldn't be entrusted with raising children, even his own grandchildren. Those older boys are a wild pair. He's a wicked man, Will."

"Martha! You know better than to believe gossip!"
Gentle Papa sounded surprisingly stern.

"Where there's that much smoke there's usually flame underneath! I don't believe those stories about his being a wrecker, but I'll warrant some of the others are true."

William, Jane's older brother, entered the conversation for the first time.

"Nat says old Rob ties a lantern to his mule and walks her along the beach on stormy nights."

"That's nonsense!" Papa exclaimed.

"Why'd he do that?" T. J. asked.

"To lure a ship in to shore. The captain thinks it's the riding lights of a moored vessel, and comes in close for safety, and then runs aground."

William's face was animated. Jane looked adoringly at him across the table. Everyone loved William. At sixteen, tall and broad-shouldered with sparkling blue eyes, he had a quality of gentleness unusual in a boy. T. J. worshipped the ground he walked, and now was hanging on every word.

"Well, go on!" he said breathlessly. "Then what?"

"Why, then, when the ship wrecks, he salvages her cargo," William replied. "Just like the old Barnegat pirates."

"Golly! Anachronistic!" T. J. whistled. "Do you think it's true?"

"Certainly not," Papa said firmly. "The old men here on the island are all born yarn-spinners. The wilder the story, the better they like it. Martha, do we have a dessert tonight?"

Mama went to the cupboard and brought a large dish of stewed prunes to the table.

18

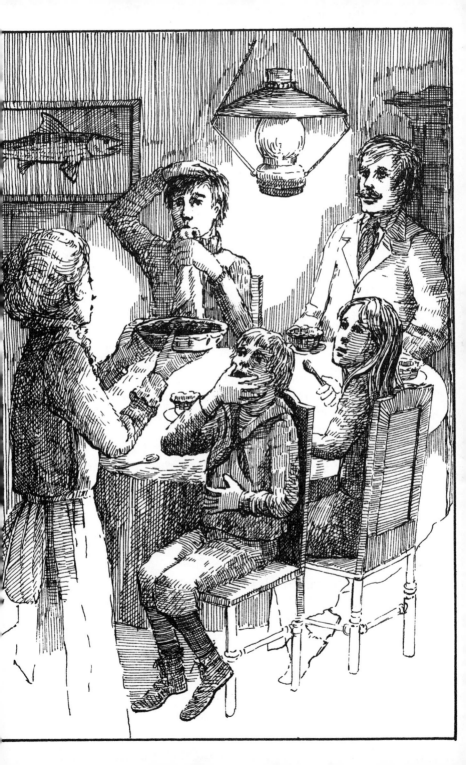

All three children groaned.

"Oh, not again!"

Mama calmly spooned the fruit into small bowls.

"No complaints, please."

Last year an Austrian vessel, the *Imperatrice Elizabetta*, had been wrecked on the treacherous Barnegat shoals. The cargo had been dried fruit from Spain, and for days afterward crates had washed ashore. The thrifty islanders had salvaged hundreds of these, and for months now every meal had featured prunes in one form or another.

Papa chuckled.

"I heard a rumor from Philadelphia. The people who come to Captain Bond's boarding house say they won't be back next summer if there are any prunes still left."

William laughed out loud.

"I heard Captain Bond had to build two new privies last summer."

"WILLIAM!"

His mother was genuinely shocked.

"I'm sorry, Mama," William mumbled, trying to hide his grin.

T. J. was doubled up, holding a napkin to his face, and Jane choked on a prune skin.

"This whole family is disgraceful!" Mama stood up, her face very red. "You are all becoming like a pack of savages!"

Papa pushed back his chair. Sensing his wife's annoyance and wishing to avoid a scene, he tactfully changed the subject.

"All right, the lot of you," he said firmly. "Get to

your chores. Martha, dear, will you please put an extra bit of coffee in the canister? It's going to be a long night."

He turned to Jane.

"Janie, will you be my Pack Rat tonight?"

She nodded happily.

"Oh, yes, Papa."

"Just don't stay up there talking," Mama warned. "I'm leaving the dishes for you to wash tonight."

The Jones children took turns at being what Papa called his Official Pack Rat. On his watch he had to carry the tall cans of kerosene to power the great light up the long, circular staircase to the top of the lighthouse tower. He couldn't manage these and his other gear too, so the children were pressed into service.

"I don't see why you can't leave some of your books up there," Mama grumbled as she began to clear the table.

"Well, I never know when I might need them," Papa replied cheerfully, pulling on an extra pair of woolen socks.

"Janie," he called over his shoulder, "get the Darwin from the top of my desk—*The Voyage of the Beagle*—the one with the green cover, and my black notebook from the top."

Papa was writing a book. During the long, lonely night watches he worked in the small room at the top of the lighthouse. His book was a biography of a Mr. Gilbert White of Selborne, England. Privately, Jane couldn't understand why in the world Papa would be interested in a long-dead and dull country parson who didn't do anything but watch birds and keep a diary.

Maybe it was because Papa loved to watch birds himself. He'd taught the children the names and habits of all the sea birds that lived on the island, and much about the curious and wonderful creatures that lived in the ocean and on the marshes. And because she loved her father, Jane knew that anything he did was important.

Carrying a lantern and her father's books, coffee and sandwiches, Jane preceded him across the windy dune to the base of the lighthouse. Together they stopped for a moment, struck silent by the beauty of the evening. Sunset flared its mad wild colors across the whole wide western sky—great sweeping strokes of indigo and slashes of scarlet, orange and apricot, with a skift of fine-layered cloud traced in silver-gilt. The bay, flat as glass, mirrored the jubilance of color.

Finally Papa spoke.

"Ought to be fine tomorrow," he observed.

"I'm glad the new girl is coming," Jane said, as her father unlocked the heavy wooden door at the base of the lighthouse.

"I hope she'll turn out to be a good friend," Papa replied. "She's had a hard time of it."

Once they were inside and had begun to climb the great spiral staircase all conversation ceased. The openwork iron steps were attached to a huge iron pole that rose straight up the center of the lighthouse shaft. They curved around like the reticulated skin of a snake, winding up and up, touching the brick sides of the lighthouse in only a few places.

Two hundred and seventeen steps!

Jane still counted them each time she went up. The

hard soles of her shoes made a faintly chiming cling-clang, and the sound echoed softly against the brick walls. The weight of Papa behind her, carrying the heavy cans of kerosene, made the slender staircase sway ever so slightly.

They paused for breath on the first platform. Here a small window faced west. The fierce crimson sun ball had nearly disappeared now.

"Papa," Jane said, "have you ever noticed how fast the dark comes? I mean, you can really see it—it sweeps in over the ocean like a big dark wing."

He smiled at her.

"Yes, it's just like that! It's because the land and the water are so flat. There's no twilight here, just light, and then night."

They began to climb once more.

The lighthouse had four windows at different levels, one at each point of the compass—North, East, South and West. The top of the tower was made entirely of glass. Up there was the great light itself, with its thousand reflecting prisms. It threw its strong warning beam far out to sea.

Coming up through a narrow hatchway they finally reached the top floor which housed the mechanism that turned the light. Even Jane was puffing as she set the lantern and books on a small table her father used for a desk.

"I wish I could stay for awhile," she said regretfully.

She loved this tiny room at the top of the world. And she loved to talk with her father. He listened a great deal, and he knew so many interesting things. He really seemed to understand about her drawing. Mama just thought it was silly and a waste of time, but Papa knew how much it meant to her.

He'd looked—really looked—at her sketch of the conch shell. Even before it was finished he said, "Yes, it's got the right curve, like the swell of a wave. It seems to rise and crest itself—like a part of the sea itself." It was just what she'd been trying to capture, and she'd felt joy surge in her.

But there was never enough time with Papa, and when he and Mama were together they formed a little world of two in which Jane had no part. It was only here, at the top of the light, that Jane felt her father belonged to her.

"Can't stay tonight, dear," her father said. "Mama has chores waiting for you."

Jane made no reply, but reluctantly kissed her father good-night. She began the long descent of the spiral staircase. It was almost dark now, and the swinging lantern sent her giant shadow dancing on the whitewashed walls.

Next time, maybe, she could stay and talk.

⸺⸕Chapter Three ⸙⸺

Next morning the big kitchen was bright with sun-
shine and smelled of blueberry pancakes frying on the
griddle. Jane had just slid into her chair at the table
when there was a loud knocking at the door.

"Will you please answer the door, Jane?" Mama
asked, busy pouring batter.

The wind caught the door, wrenching it from her
grasp, and flung it with a loud crash against the wall.

Jane found herself looking into two sparkling brown
eyes.

"Hullo there! Here I am—all ready for some
teachin'."

The girl standing on the porch was small, just about
Jane's height, with an untidy mop of dark brown curls.
Her plump figure was draped in an incredibly dirty
red shawl with tattered fringe, and her long black

dress, greenish with age, was wrinkled beyond belief and billowing in the wind. She looked like a young and slightly wicked witch.

"H—hello," Jane stammered. "You must be Dolly Speers."

Mama, turning from the stove, and William and T. J. at the table, were staring in astonishment at the girl as she stepped over the doorsill and into the room.

"My goodness!" Mama said. "We weren't expecting you so early! Have you had your breakfast?"

"No, m'am—an' I'm mighty hungry."

"Where's your grandfather? Didn't he bring you?"

"No, m'am. I come shank's mare. Gran'pap's home asleep, drunker'n a coot," Dolly replied cheerfully.

She sat down in the chair William offered her, next to Jane's.

"My, this's nice!" she exclaimed, beaming at all of them.

Mama's face was very red.

"Well," she said crisply, "here—have some griddle cakes."

She thrust a heaping plate in front of Dolly.

Jane was staring at the girl with curiosity. She'd never seen anyone like her before, and she wasn't quite sure how she felt.

Dolly gobbled the blueberry pancakes hungrily, spilling syrup down the front of her already stained dress. As she ate she kept up a running line of chatter, smiling artfully at William as she talked.

"Say, this's the best grub I've et in months! You're certain sure a fine cook, Miz Jones! Efen you teach as good as you cook, I oughter learn pretty fast.

26

"Gran'pap, he's set on me gettin' some schoolin', though I sez, what's a girl got need of readin' an' writin' for anyways? Jest to get married an' have a houseful of babies?"

For the first time in her life Jane saw her mother at a loss for words. William and T. J. were silent, struggling not to laugh. She knew the look, when they were just bursting inside and trying not to show it. Suddenly Jane felt protective. She didn't want them making fun of her new friend.

"When you've finished eating," she said to Dolly, "I'll show you around outside."

Mama seemed relieved to see them go.

"Be back in half an hour for lessons," was all that she said.

If we're going to be friends, thought Jane, I might as well start out right.

"Come on," she said, once they were out of the house, "I'll show you one of my favorite places."

She began to run across the dunes, with Dolly following.

They made their way through little thickets of bayberry bushes growing scattered over the sandy hillocks. In summer Jane loved to snap the glossy leaves and sniff their aromatic fragrance. In the autumn they gathered the tiny silver berries to boil for wax, and made sweet-smelling candles. Now the bushes were starred with dark red buds.

At some distance down the beach where the dunes rose steep, and out of sight of the big house, lay a huge pile of giant rocks. They looked like some long prehistoric monster crouched on the sand. They were not native to the island, but had been brought over by the Army Engineers when they built the lighthouse twelve years ago. These rocks were left over, and had been carted down the beach and left to the sea and the shifting sands.

Jane climbed over the largest rock and dropped down to the soft sand below. Here the rocks made a tiny roofless cave.

"Isn't this nice? Nobody ever comes here but me."

Dolly didn't seem awfully impressed. She leaned back against the rock wall and stretched out her legs. Jane noticed that there were holes in the soles of her scuffed shoes.

"Is your mum crabby?"

"Crabby?" Jane was puzzled.

"You know—kind of mean and bossy?"

Jane felt a prick of loyalty.

"Oh, no. She's—well, she's awfully keen on manners, and doing your duty, and being obedient and stuff like that. But she's not mean."

"That's good," Dolly said. "I kinda have a feelin' she don't like me."

"Of course she likes you! Why golly, she doesn't even know you yet."

"Yeah, that's true. Say, your big brother's awful good-lookin', ain't he!"

"William? Yes, isn't he! And he's nice too! You'll like William."

"Does he have schoolin' with us?"

"No, he's too old. He helps Captain Cranmer on his fishing boat, and goes clamming. He's going to college in the fall, and Papa's tutoring him in Greek and Latin."

"You sure got a smart family," Dolly observed.

"Well, you see, Papa taught at the University of Pennsylvania till he got asthma, and they gave him a long leave of absence. That's why we came here—for the sea air. He's a lot better now, and I guess we'll be going back to Philadelphia to live in a year or so.

"I don't think about that very much," Jane went on confidentially. "I don't want to go back. I just love it here so much! I'd like to live here on the island for the whole rest of my life!"

"You crazy or somethin'? Philadelphia—now there's a place! Lots of things to see an' do, an' shops an' everythin'! That's the place for me!"

"I don't remember it much," Jane said. "I was only seven when we came to the island. I'm twelve now—I'll be thirteen in August. Have you lived here long?"

"Only 'bout a year. My mum left us—she went off with an actor-man. That was down in Richmond. So Gran'pap, he took us, me an' my brothers, an' we been livin' with him."

Dolly pulled the tattered shawl closer about her shoulders.

"Richmond was nice," she said reflectively. "Someday I'm goin' back there, or to Philadelphia. . . ."

Impulsively Jane reached out and touched her grubby hand.

"I'm glad you're here now," she said softly. "And we can be friends."

Dolly smiled at her.

"Yeah, that'll be fun. Only I don't know how I'll take to this learnin' stuff."

29

"I'll help you," Jane offered. "It's not so bad, really, except maybe for algebra—and William helps me with that."

She returned Dolly's smile, suddenly feeling very happy. There was a dashing quality about Dolly, a who-cares attitude that Jane found new and exciting, even a little dangerous. She seemed to be all the things Jane longed to be—free and unhampered. She's going to be fun, Jane thought.

"I guess we'd better be getting back now," Jane said regretfully.

They scrambled to their feet.

"Yeah," Dolly agreed. "Don't want to make a bad impression the first day out!"

Jane thought briefly of the look on Mama's face when she first saw Dolly, and wondered.

"Race you to the house," she cried.

-ᗪ Chapter Four ᗷ-

Three weeks had gone by with amazing swiftness. Dolly came each morning, sometimes walking and sometimes riding her grandfather's old mule. Her 'schoolin', however, was not an outstanding success so far. Jane was continually amazed at Dolly's ingenuity in thinking up excuses for not doing her lessons.

"I jest had to shuck a whole tub o' clams last night," she'd said to Mama, "an' my pore fingers was too sore to hold a pencil. . . ."

Or she'd say, "Laws! That no-good brother o' mine! He took my readin' book an' hid it on me—put it behind the cracker tin, would you believe? He's a real trial to me, Miz Jones. . . ."

Even when Mama spoke sharply it seemed to make no difference to Dolly. She'd just grin cheerfully.

This morning the schoolroom was very quiet. Dust motes danced in a butter-colored patch of sun on the

31

work table. Jane looked up from the algebra problem with which she was struggling over to where Betsy Lippencott sat. Her neat head bent, her pencil was flying across the paper.

I just hate people who can do algebra fast, Jane thought bitterly. She's nothing but trouble for me.

As she watched Betsy, Jane's mind went back to last week. Jane and Dolly had planned to go shell hunting on the beach one afternoon. They had just started down the porch steps when Betsy came out of the house.

"Where're you going?" she asked.

Dolly glanced at Jane and frowned.

"Oh," Jane replied, hesitating, "nowhere special—"

"I want to come too." Betsy edged nearer.

Dolly made a face behind her back, and Jane couldn't help giggling.

"Oh, you wouldn't have any fun. We're—we're going to do our reading lessons together," Jane said.

Betsy stamped her foot.

"You're just a big liar, Jane Jones!"

Now Jane was angry.

"I am not! Why don't you mind your own business!"

"You two think you're so smart," Betsy howled. "Always going off together. I saw you up at the top of the lighthouse yesterday. You're not allowed to go up there. I'm going to tell—"

They were making such a racket they hadn't noticed Mama standing in the doorway.

"What's going on here?" she demanded.

"Oh, Mrs. Jones"—Betsy ran to her side—"they won't play with me. They never want to play with me."

Mama looked at Jane, but before she could speak Jane tossed her head.

"Oh, all right," she said crossly to Betsy. "We're only going for a walk on the beach. You can come if you want to."

She and Dolly started off down the path across the dunes without a backward glance.

This little incident had cost Jane a scolding and a lecture on manners that night, and further settled her resolve to avoid Betsy whenever possible.

Now, here was Betsy working diligently, while Jane's paper was a mass of crossed-out errors.

Across the room at a smaller table by the window, Clara Lippencott and T. J. were copying spelling words onto their slates. Mama sat at her desk going over their history exams with the older Lippencott boys.

By herself in a big chair by the window Dolly sat, a Fourth Grade reader open in her lap. She was not looking at it, however, but stared moodily out of the window. Noticing Jane, she threw her a broad wink. Jane returned it and then quickly bent her head to the troublesome algebra.

They had planned a picnic for that afternoon, and there had been the problem of how to get rid of Betsy.

"I just know she'll want to tag along," Jane had complained, "and Mama will say we have to take her."

"Well, she's no fun—jest a big tattletale, an' we don't want her along," Dolly had said. "So jest don't even tell your mum. I know—say you've got to go down to ol' Miz Cranmer's, to help her or somethin'. I'll head off home like always, an' then we can meet down the road a 'ways."

It was a devious arrangement, and involved a lot of secret planning. Jane was not used to deception, but she found a guilty little thrill in it, and finally they had the plan worked out.

The long morning dragged interminably. Jane was scolded for having six problems wrong out of ten, and then Mama patiently went over each one of them with her again. But finally the hands on the schoolroom clock pointed to twelve, and the children knew they were free for the rest of the day.

Jane, not used to lying, did it badly. She stammered and her face grew red, but Mama seemed preoccupied and didn't notice. So an hour later Jane was flying down the road to meet Dolly.

The object of today's exploration was to be the forest at Harvey Cedars. The road, a sandy track that went straight down the center of the island, was skirted on either side by the cedar swamp.

At high tide it was marshy, but on the ebb tide it was possible to walk through in places. Though the old wind-gnarled trees were not tall, it was the nearest thing to a woodland on the island, and this darkly mysterious place had long been a source of fascination to Jane.

"Let's wait, and eat when we get to the woods," Jane said, when she finally caught up with Dolly.

She had filched bread and cheese and some cookies from the pantry, and four withered winter-stored apples, and had hidden them under her coat.

They tramped along the deserted road together under a bright April sky.

"It must be awful—havin' to account for yourself all

the time," Dolly observed. "Gran'pap's not much, but at least he don't ask questions all the time."

"It's terrible," Jane sighed in agreement. "It's do this, and do that—all the time! It's 'Wash your hands, Jane,' and 'Jane, put that sketchbook away,' and 'Make your bed, Jane.' I get so everlasting sick of it!"

"Your mum's a fair corker, I will say. Don't she never let up?"

"Never!" Jane replied gloomily.

She was about to say, "I wish she'd let me go around like you. I wish I didn't have to keep clean all the time, and watch my language—"

Then she quickly thought that wouldn't sound kind, and she didn't want to hurt her friend. For the truth of it was, though Jane would never have admitted this, that part of the reason she liked Dolly so much was because Mama didn't like her. Mama thought Dolly was rude and rough and dirty. Jane had heard her saying so to Papa.

Jane was fascinated by Dolly. She admired her free-and-easy manners, her don't-give-a-darn attitude toward grown-ups, her cheekiness and her courage in doing and saying exactly what she felt. She wished she could be like that herself.

"Hey, look! We're almost there," Dolly cried.

Here and there, from the road's edge, a faint trail was visible through the close-growing pines. They chose one of the little sandy paths, and were soon in among the cedar trees, which caught at their coats with scratchy grasping fingers. It was so quiet they could hear the distant boom of the surf on the beach.

They sat together on a fallen log and divided the

food. It tasted wonderful, and they hungrily devoured everything Jane had brought. As she was brushing the last crumbs from her skirt, Jane noticed a tiny flash of white fluttering among the thick-set cedars.

"Oh, look," she cried, jumping to her feet. "I wonder. . . ."

She began pushing her way through the branches. Dolly followed her.

"Hey," she cried. "There's another one!"

A short distance away another scrap of cloth glimmered like a tiny signal flag.

There was no path here, but farther on ahead they could see still another marker.

"It's a trail," Jane shouted. "Let's follow it!"

The low-slung branches made difficult going, and in places they were forced to crawl on their hands and knees. But it was definitely leading somewhere, for the little scraps of white continued to beckon the way deeper into the swamp. They were almost through the band of trees, for ahead they could see the ocean glittering with sun sparks.

Suddenly, without warning, they came upon a little clearing. In its center was what appeared to be a great mound of pine boughs.

"Cripes! It looks like a grave!" Dolly said in awe.

Jane, swallowing her fear, walked nearer.

"My golly," she breathed. "It's a boat!"

The branches had been loosely laid to form a rough cover, and they quickly pulled them off. It was indeed a boat, a long surfboat, not like the flat-nosed garveys that were used on the bay. It glistened with fresh paint, and in the bottom they could see several objects wrapped neatly in oilskins.

"Let's see what's in it," Jane suggested, clambering over the side.

As she bent to untie the hemp rope that bound the oilskin, a piece of paper fluttered down. It bore no writing, only a crudely drawn skull and crossbones.

Dolly was peering over her shoulder.

"Hey—what's that?"

Jane studied the drawing thoughtfully.

"It's William's," she said finally. "I'm sure of it."

She turned to Dolly.

"He always puts this mark on something he doesn't want anyone to touch—like his penknife, or his bird book or even if he has a piece of pie he wants to save. It's like a warning thing."

"You mean the boat belongs to him?"

"I don't know." Jane was puzzled. "He never said anything about it."

"Well, let's open the oilskins."

"Maybe we shouldn't—"

"Oh, come on—we've gone this far. . . ." Dolly was tugging at the knots.

The oilskin wrappings unfolded to reveal four long wooden-handled objects with sharp steel points.

"Harpoons!" Jane cried.

"What's that?"

"They're—well, they're sort of like special spears. They're used to kill whales," Jane explained.

Papa had shown her pictures of these weapons used in the whaling trade.

"Pooh," Dolly scoffed. "No one catches whales around here."

"But they used to," Jane said. "Old Captain Cranmer used to go whaling. He told us. They kept

their longboats on the beach and they had a whale-watch. It was a big pole with a platform on the top. When he was a boy he said he used to sit up there and watch the ocean till he saw a whale spouting way out, and then he'd call—"

Jane suddenly stopped. She remembered T. J. sitting up in the tree. Could it be? Oh, but that was silly! William and T. J. wouldn't try to take off after a whale all by themselves! But still. . . .

The bottom of the boat yielded, as well as the harpoons, several coils of new strong rope, three sets of oars and a small package containing a can of fresh water, several packets of stonelike sea biscuits and a small, odorous wheel of cheese. There was also an old compass, carefully wrapped.

"We've got to put these back exactly as we found them," Jane told Dolly. "I'll try to find out what's going on."

"Well, I think the whole thing's kinda dumb," Dolly grumbled, helping her to rewrap the articles. "I thought maybe we was goin' to find a real treasure, like jewels or somethin'."

"They say Captain Kidd buried treasure here on the island," Jane said, carefully retying the ropes and replacing the paper with the skull and crossbones on top. "William and the Lippencott boys have dug a lot of holes all over, hunting for it—"

"Now that'd be a worthwhile find! Not just a dumb old boat."

"Well, it's still a mystery," Jane said cheerfully. "And I do love a good mystery. I'll let you know what I can find out. . . ."

-⊸ Chapter Five ⊷-

As Jane approached home late that afternoon, dark clouds were already gathering. The bright April sky had vanished and now was threatening with storm. The wind had veered around to the northeast, and gulls were screaming and sweeping low over the big house.

Mama stood on the porch looking anxiously toward the road, her long skirt billowing in the rising wind. When she saw Jane the look of relief on her face was immediately replaced with a frown.

"Where have you been, young lady?"

Jane climbed the porch step slowly.

"I—"

"You told me you were going down to visit Mrs. Cranmer."

"Well, I—"

"Mrs. Cranmer was here this afternoon, to pay a call. She hadn't seen hide nor hair of you!"

Jane looked miserably at her shoes.

"You were off with that Dolly Speers again, weren't you?"

"Y-yes, Mama. We—we just went down to the woods. . . ."

"Oh, Jane! Whatever am I to do with you? You know how I feel about that girl, but what is worse, you lied!"

Mama grasped her arm.

"Come in out of the wind and have your supper."

Supper was a gloomy meal. Jane, feeling resentful and angry, did not raise her eyes from her plate. She didn't even taste the food. Mama was quick and cross with everyone, and even William and T. J. kept silent. Papa was visibly worried.

"We're in for a big blow tonight, I'm afraid," he said. "I've seldom seen the barometer drop so fast. I think I'll stand watch with John tonight. I just have a funny feeling in my bones."

The wind was howling like a thousand demons, and before they had finished supper a tattoo of rain was peppering the window glass.

One of Mama's rules regarding punishment was never to withhold food. No matter how serious the misbehavior, the Jones children were never sent to bed without supper.

"Growing children need nourishment" was one of her maxims.

But Mama had other ingenious ways of exacting repentance. She seemed to have an uncanny knowledge of just what you hated to do most, Jane had noticed. So

41

she was not surprised when after the table had been cleared Mama handed her the sewing basket and a pile of socks.

"Take these to your room and darn them," she said sternly. "I'll be up to talk to you later."

Jane dared not approach William privately to ask about the hidden boat. She was in enough trouble already. So she meekly took the basket and a kerosene lamp from the shelf and climbed the staircase to her room.

Being the only girl in the family did have certain advantages, the chief one being having a room of her own. It was the smallest bedroom, and faced east overlooking the ocean. There was a high four-poster bed with a deep, soft feather mattress, and a little table at the window where Jane kept her drawing things and her books.

On shelves Papa had built for her, Jane had arranged her special treasures—the huge pink and cream conch shell, and a lovely bit of driftwood that she had decorated with small shells, bits of ferny dried seaweed and a little gull William had carved for her. There was a fat glass jar filled with fragments of beach glass she had found, which sparkled in the sun like rare jewels, a vase of feathery marsh-grass plumes and a row of dolls she no longer played with but could not bear to discard. The walls were covered with her own sketches, tacked up with drawing pins. Next to the top of the lighthouse, Jane loved her own room more than any place in the world.

But tonight, shut away from the rest of the family, with the storm crashing about the house, Jane felt lonely as she worked at the detested darning. She could hear voices and doors opening and closing as the long evening dragged on interminably. Several times, with a sinking heart, she thought she heard Mama's footsteps on the stairs, but the dreaded knock at her door did not come.

Jane had nearly finished the next-to-last sock when she heard shouting from outside the house, above the wild moaning of the wind. She ran to the window, trying in vain to peer out into the surrounding darkness. Dimly, through the slashing rain, she could see lights in the dooryard.

Above and beyond the big house the long beam of the light from the lighthouse sliced through the heavy rain. Jane struggled to open the sticking window sash and when it finally leaped up almost of its own accord a fierce wind caught the curtain, lashing it out viciously. Cold rain slapped her face.

The door at the base of the lighthouse flew open and in a pale swash of lantern light Jane could see her father.

"It's true," he shouted. "A ship's going down out there—just beyond the inlet!"

Jane could now make out a group of men gathered in the dooryard. Blown on the wind she could hear the whinnying of their horses tied to the rail at the side of the house. She could recognize the figure of George Inman, the third lighthouse keeper. George was a young man of twenty who lived with his new wife, Mary, in a little cottage near the big house.

Old Captain Cranmer was there, his long white beard streaming out over his oilskin slicker, and several other men she knew from farther down the island. They formed a self-appointed life-saving crew, and the sailors from many a foundering vessel owed their lives to this small band of dedicated men.

"We can't get through that surf," one man shouted. "She's proper fierce tonight! You sure there's a ship out there, Will?"

"Pretty certain," Papa replied. "With this muck it's hard to tell for sure, but I saw her riding lights earlier this evening. I think she was making for the inlet for shelter."

"God help 'er! That captain must be a damn fool," Captain Cranmer shouted. "Wind's wrong for comin' in."

"Let's give it a try," George Inman cried. "If we can just get a line out to 'er. . . ."

"She's too far out for the Lyle gun. Now, boy, jest hear that white water roarin'—we'd never make it." The old captain's voice was gruff. "Best to wait till first light. She'll hold that long if she's any size. . . ."

Jane could see the group move toward the house, and heard them come into the kitchen. She knew Mama would make a big pot of coffee and make a place for the men to rest until dawn. Then they would make an attempt to rescue the foundering vessel.

She was soaking wet from the rain that blew in the open window, but once again she tried to peer out to sea. The whole world seemed to be a roaring, howling pit of blackness. Try as she might, she could see no prick of light that might be the troubled ship.

Finally Jane closed the window. She dried herself, slipped into her long flannel nightgown, blew out the

44

lamp and climbed hurriedly into her warm soft bed. She scrunched up her toes to warm them and snuggled deep into the feather mattress.

She loved this cozy cave, safe behind walls, against the buffeting winds and the fury of the storm. She liked to think that she was here, at the outermost edge of the North American continent, with no land until the far coast of Spain. Storms were scary, but they were exciting too, especially when you were safely tucked in a feather bed. Winds charged the house like an attacking horde of demons.

Jane burrowed deeper, feeling guiltily grateful. Mama would be too busy with the men to come up for her scolding. Tomorrow would be time enough to worry about that. Jane said a little prayer for the men on the ship and drifted off to sleep.

-*{Chapter Six}*-

Her window was just a faint smear of gray when Jane awakened. She could hear voices downstairs and smell the rich aroma of frying fish. Rubbing her eyes sleepily she sat up.

Then she remembered the ship!

The floorboards felt icy beneath her bare feet as she raced to the window. In the cold morning light the sea looked like dusty pewter. It was churning fearfully and, sure enough, there out beyond the breakwater at the inlet's mouth a ship tilted drunkenly.

Her father and the other men were already on the beach. Two surfboats were poised, ready to plunge into the crashing surf. The Lyle gun, which looked like a small cannon, was in position on the beach, a wooden bucket of coiled rope beside it. The rope was attached to the nose of a little rocket. When fired it would carry a lifeline out to the sinking ship.

Over the sound of the wind and the surf Jane heard the hollow boom of the gun as match was touched to gunpowder, and saw the rocket shoot through the air.

"Damn! She missed!" she heard one of the men shout. "She's too far out. . . ."

"We'll have to take the boat," another man shouted.

Jane could see the men in their oilskin coats and big sou'wester hats begin pushing one of the boats into the foaming surf. The breakers were at least twelve feet high, and Jane could see the boat hesitate and pitch as the men clambered in and grabbed the oars.

Golly, I'd better hurry, Jane thought. She scrambled into her clothes quickly and ran downstairs. As she burst into the kitchen T. J., a half-eaten slice of bread clenched between his teeth, was struggling into his coat.

"I'm goin' to the beach," he cried. "Come on —hurry!"

Mama was not visible anywhere, so Jane grabbed her coat from the peg on the wall and followed T. J. out the door.

The wind, though still high, was not as strong as the previous night and the rain had nearly stopped.

"Oh, T. J! Look!"

Jane grasped her brother's sleeve and pointed.

Across the dooryard, at the base of the lighthouse, was a pitiful sight. At least twenty great feathered bodies lay like drifted snow. The sea gulls had flown or been blown into the glass sides at the top of the light. Their necks broken, they had fallen lifeless to the ground.

"Creepers! How anachronistic!" T. J. breathed in

47

awe. "That's more than I've ever seen before! That must have been some storm!"

"There's almost too many for a funeral," Jane said.

She felt a slow, aching sadness as she gazed at the beautiful birds, so sodden and still in death.

"We can dig a great big pit, and have one funeral for all of 'em," T. J. said practically.

It had been their custom to hold funerals for the dead birds they found from time to time. They carefully dug the small graves, held a simple ceremony with hymn-singing, and marked the little mounds lovingly with sprigs of bayberry, wild roses in season or the great pink marshmallow blooms. Jane always wore an old black veil of her mother's, and was usually the one who made the simple speech over the dead. Betsy and Clara sometimes joined in, only they always pretended to cry and howl and wail, and made a terrible commotion.

"That's how all the ladies acted at my aunt's funeral," Betsy had explained, "and then we had a lovely big dinner afterward."

"Well, this is different," Jane had told her crossly. "This is birds, not people. And I think you ought to cry softly, if you're going to cry at all."

Jane had never been to a real person's funeral, but she had heard the grown-ups talk about it, and she knew how to conduct such an affair. She also felt that it was somehow disrespectful to the dead to carry on so.

T. J. interrupted her thoughts about a mass funeral for the sea gulls.

"Come on, Jane. Let's go down to the beach."

Sam, after sniffing at the dead birds, had rejoined them. He began to bark as they ran down across the dunes.

They could see the rescue boat far out now, in rough water, but beyond the dangerous breakers at the shore. It looked like a tiny chip of wood tossing on the vast expanse of the angry sea.

The sinking ship was tilting more steeply now. Her prow rose out of the churning water like the sharp beak of an enormous bird.

"It says—the *John H. Hoyt*," T. J. said, squinting to see the name painted on the side. "Ever hear of it?"

"No," Jane answered.

She was peering, trying to see if any of the crew were on deck. She thought she saw some moving specks, but the ship was too far away to be sure.

Sam, having investigated the abandoned Lyle gun, was now running off down the beach. T. J. stared after him.

"What's gotten into that dog?" he asked, half to himself.

He turned to Jane.

"Look at Sam! He looks like he's tracking something."

Jane glanced where he was pointing. Sam, his nose to the sand, his black plumy tail wagging, was heading rapidly down the beach.

"Maybe we ought to follow him," T. J. suggested.

"All right," Jane agreed.

There was nothing going on just now. It would be some time before the rescue boat returned, and if she went home she'd just have to face Mama.

They walked a long distance down the beach together, keeping the black dog in sight. The tide was ebbing, and at the high-water mark, nearly up to the dunes, the sand was littered with sea wrack. Timbers lay helter-skelter, and great mounds of clam shells and tangled kelp.

"We'll have to come back later and see if we can find anything really anachronistic," T. J. said.

A storm at sea left many strange and wonderful things tossed upon the sand.

"T. J.—Look!" Jane cried suddenly.

She pointed to the smooth sand at their feet.

Footprints.

Quite a number of them led up from the water's edge. It looked as if something heavy had been dragged along, and there were a few ominous reddish-brown stains on the sand.

T. J. squatted down to examine the marks. Then he gazed up at Jane.

"Blood?" he whispered.

She nodded fearfully.

"Could be—"

Just then they heard a frantic barking. The sound came from the edge of the cedar grove where T. J.'s shanty stood. Sam was running around the shanty in circles, barking wildly. Jane and T. J. began to run.

Before they reached the shanty the little door flew open and a large, bearded man stepped out.

"Ahoy, there!" he called, waving to them.

The children were panting by the time they reached him. The bearded man was patting Sam, who wagged his tail happily. The man walked out to meet Jane and T. J.

"You young 'uns live hereabouts?" he called.

"Yes, sir," Jane replied.

"Good," the man sighed. "We got us some trouble—one of our crew is hurt bad in there."

He gestured toward the shack.

"Is that your ship?" T. J. asked, pointing out to sea.

"Yep, lad. That's her. Or what's left of her—"

"Oh! But—" Jane cried suddenly, "they've gone out to rescue you. . . ."

The bearded man stared out across the water. The tiny surfboat was all but lost to sight in the deep trough of a wave.

"By gar!" he exclaimed, and then turned to the children. "We made it in last night—a fearful thing it were, too! But we didn't lose a man."

He looked at Jane.

"Is your pappy in that boat?"

"Yes sir," she replied, "and all the rescue squad. They couldn't get through the surf last night, and you were too far out for the Lyle gun, and—"

She broke off helplessly.

"Well, now—let's try to send 'em a signal," the bearded man said. "You skin on home an' tell your mam, or whoever's there. An' try to git us a stretcher or somethin'. Our fellow can't walk."

By this time several other men had appeared at the door of the shanty. They were soaked to the skin with sea water, and shivering with the cold.

"We'll get help right away," Jane promised.

She and T. J. began to run back toward the big house.

--•≼Chapter Seven≽•--

Jane's chest hurt and her legs ached from running. They could see Mama standing on the widow's walk on the roof of the big house. She was watching the rescue boat through Papa's long spyglass.

The rain had begun again, and the wind was once more rising.

"Mama! Mama. . . ." T. J. shouted, but she couldn't hear him.

They raced into the house and pounded up the stairs to the attic. A tiny door led out onto the widow's walk, which was a small fenced platform on the roof of the house. It was called a widow's walk because the wives of sea captains often waited and watched there for their husbands' ships to come in. And because oftentimes the men were lost at sea, the little lookouts had been given their sad name.

Mama wheeled about as they stepped out onto the platform.

"Where have you two been—?" She stopped, seeing their faces.

"Oh, Mama," Jane panted, "the ship's crew are in T.J.'s shanty and one of them is hurt real bad, and they need help. And someone's got to warn the rescue boat, and—"

Mama hesitated for only a second.

"Run and get me a bedsheet quickly," she commanded.

Jane scurried back to her room, stripped a sheet from her bed and carried it back up to the roof.

"Now, you and T. J. each take a corner—hold on or you'll lose it in this wind!—and wave it. I only hope they'll see it from the boat," Mama said. "Mrs. Lippencott and I will take some blankets down to the shanty, and see what can be done for those poor men. . . ."

And Mama was gone.

It took all of their strength and ingenuity to hang on to the bedsheet. It was flapping and straining like one of the huge white snow geese that flew over the island in winter.

After a struggle, Jane was able to tie one corner of the sheet around her left wrist, and this gave her a free hand. She lifted the heavy spyglass Mama had left behind and adjusted it awkwardly to her eye.

Through the powerful glass the churning sea leaped up in front of her. She could see each towering wave as it rolled in. Moving the cylinder slowly she finally brought the lifeboat into focus in its round glass eye.

Almost as clearly as if she were there in the boat with them, Jane could see her father and William and George Inman, each pulling at one of the long oars. There were eight men at the oars altogether, straining against the mighty pull of the rough seas. Captain Cranmer stood in the prow.

Suddenly he swung around and pointed.

"Oh T. J.," Jane cried, "I think maybe they see us."

"I sure hope so," T. J. grumbled. "I'm gettin' awful tired."

"Well, hang on, 'cause I'm not sure."

Jane, from her vantage point on the roof, could now see Mama and Mrs. Lippencott struggling against the wind, making their way down the beach. They were carrying blankets and poles to make a stretcher. She could also see young Mary Inman, George's wife, come out of her cottage door carrying a large iron kettle. Mary was expecting her first baby to be born early in the summer, and she moved slowly and heavily in the wind.

Mary made her way toward the big house, and Jane knew that she would go into the kitchen downstairs and begin making soup and hot tea for the men.

Jane's arm ached with the pull of the billowing sheet, but once again she lifted the spyglass.

"They're turning the lifeboat," she called to T. J. "They're starting back. I'm sure they've seen us now."

"Good!" he sighed. "Let's put this thing down."

"No, we'd better not, just in case."

"But, Jane, my arm hurts!"

"Well, so does mine," she said, and then added: "Please, T. J.—just a little longer."

"All right. But let me look once."

"Here—I'll hold it to your eye for you."

It took some doing to hang onto the sheet and hold the heavy spyglass for T. J., and to get it focused on the pitching boat.

"I'm gettin' dizzy," he complained. "Oh, wait—now it's all right. Oh, my gosh! Jane! Jane! *It's tipped over!*"

T. J.'s voice rose to a wail.

Jane strained frantically to see through the blowing rain. The boat had reached the pounding breakers in near the shore. Jane saw a huge wave slap it sideways. The prow lifted high, balanced for a breath-gripping second and then smashed downward.

The men were flung helter-skelter out into the wild white water. From this distance they looked like rag dolls flying in all directions.

Jane felt sick panic fill her throat.

She dropped the spyglass and tore at the sheet tied to her wrist.

"Hurry!" she cried.

She never remembered later how fast she had run down the stairs. Her coat was soaked from the rain, and her long golden hair was plastered flat against her head.

She burst into the kitchen, startling Mary Inman, who was standing by the stove.

"Oh, Mary," she screamed. "The boat's overturned! Come quick!"

Mary's face drained of all color. Without a word she grabbed her shawl and followed Jane and T. J.

When they reached the beach they could see the

men from the lifeboat floating in the tumbling surf. Their cork-filled life jackets kept them afloat. With the waves' pushing, the men were staggering ashore slowly and painfully.

Jane was running toward Papa when she saw, a short distance out in the water, one man still bobbing up and down, making no effort to get in to shore. Papa had seen him too, and he began to wade back into the bone-chilling water.

Fighting the surf, Papa finally reached the man and grasped him under the arms. Then he began to make his way, stumbling and falling, back to shore with his burden.

Jane was conscious of a low, strangled cry beside her.

"It's George."

Mary began to run toward Papa.

"George! George. . . ."

Now, Jane could see Mama and Mrs. Lippencott and the men from the wrecked ship running toward them from down the beach.

Suddenly the whole beach seemed to be filled with people, shouting and milling about. It was a nightmare of confusion. Heavy rain pelted them and the cruel wind howled like a mad thing and without mercy.

--≪ Chapter Eight ≫--

The little Methodist church in the mainland town of Barnegat was quiet, even though it was filled with people. Sun poured through the colored glass window and stained Jane's hands with lovely shades of violet and rose.

At the front of the church a plain pine coffin rested on trestles draped in black. A single spray of golden forsythia blossoms lay on its top. Fluttering like a flock of tiny birds through the rafters, thin reedy notes from the little pump organ broke the afternoon silence. The organist was playing the old hymn tune "Nearer My God to Thee."

The minister, solemn in black serge, stood up in the pulpit.

"Men who go down to the sea in ships," he began gravely, "shall know the mighty works of the Lord. . . ."

Jane was thinking about George Inman, whose body lay in the coffin, and about Mary and the baby yet to be born. Jane hadn't known George well, and so his death did not leave her with a deep personal sense of loss or grief. Mary, very white and still, sat beside Jane's mother in the pew. She had no family of her own, and since the accident Mama had looked after her.

This was Jane's first real funeral and she was anxious to behave properly. She folded her hands tightly together and bent her head, avoiding the mute dark slash of the coffin.

More than George, it was the thought of dying itself which now occupied Jane's thoughts. She remembered the shock and grief of the people on the beach when it was first discovered that George was dead of a broken neck.

"He must've been struck by an oar when we was throwed out of the boat," old Captain Cranmer had surmised.

"And all for nothing!" Jane had heard John Lippencott say to Papa in a low voice. "When the crew was already safe inshore."

Jane was thinking about the night after George's death. She had felt in the way all day. Every time she tried to do or say something she was shushed up, or sent on a useless errand.

Finally, toward nightfall, she climbed the stairs and shut herself in her room. Darkness had come early, and the storm had nearly blown itself out. The *John H. Hoyt* still lurched on the shoal in rough seas, but a tugboat was due in the morning to pull her off.

The crew members had been fed and the wounded man was being nursed by Mama and Mrs. Lippencott. Papa and the other men were making arrangements to sail the ship's crew to the mainland. Mary had shut herself away in her cottage.

Jane and T. J. had hurriedly dug a large hole and buried the sea gulls without ceremony. Somehow it hadn't seemed right to hold their usual services when George's body, wrapped in a winding-sheet, lay on the bed in the spare room.

Jane, her face in her hands, sat by the window watching the night come in. She felt lonely and a little frightened.

There was a soft tap at her door.

When she opened it, there stood Papa, a kerosene lamp in one hand and a steaming mug of cocoa in the other.

"May I come in, Janie?"

"Oh, yes, Papa."

Suddenly she threw her arms about his waist and hid her face against the rough wool of his coat. He set the lamp and the cocoa on the table, and circled her with his strong arms.

Jane couldn't remember afterward all the things they had talked about that evening. But she did remember one.

"Papa," she had asked, "what does it mean . . . to die? What really happens when someone is dead?"

"That's the greatest mystery in the world, dear," he had replied. "Since the beginning of time man has pondered it."

He held her hand, sitting beside her on the bed.

"I do know that it's as much a part of life as being

born," he said slowly. "Think of something for a minute. Suppose there were no death—suppose everything went on living forever. Why, there wouldn't be room on earth for anything new! Forests would be all choked and thick if the trees didn't die. The sea would be thick with fish, and the sky all dark and heavy with birds so the sun couldn't get through. There wouldn't have been room for you, or T. J. or William—or even for Mama and me."

He was talking quietly, almost as if to himself.

"Remember how I taught you about the delicate balance of nature? How everything is so finely and magnificently ordered that each thing, no matter how small, is dependent upon others? It seems cruel; indeed, it is cruel. But it seems to be a necessity and something we have to accept."

Papa went on.

"Did you ever think, Janie, how life would be if there were no contrasts? How would you know you are happy if you'd never been sad? If you didn't ever have to work, a holiday would be no fun—it would be just like any other day."

Jane considered this thoughtfully.

"I guess you're right, Papa," she said finally. "Why, if I didn't have to do algebra, and hate it so much, drawing wouldn't be as much fun. Yes, I see what you mean!"

"And think about love," Papa had gone on, carried away by his own thoughts. "If you knew that the people you love would be with you forever—why, then, maybe you wouldn't care as deeply or show your love as much."

"Mary loved George a lot," Jane said thoughtfully.

"She used to hold his hand when they walked down the beach together. And once I saw her kiss him, on the porch of the cottage."

Papa sighed.

"Yes, dear. Mary will be very lonely. And we must help her all we can. Soon her baby will be born, and then she'll have a part of George to love, and she'll love the baby for itself. . . ."

Later that night, as she snuggled deep into her feather mattress, Jane felt much better. She still didn't understand about being dead, but she knew that Papa had told her the truth, and that was a good feeling.

Now, here in the church, the simple pageantry of the funeral seemed to make death even more unreal. Everyone seemed so busy with the ritual—the hymn-singing, the sermon and then the solemn processional walk to the graveyard.

As the coffin was lowered into the earth, a blackbird sitting on a nearby bush gave a long, sweet whistle, clear and compelling.

Why, it's almost as if George is being welcomed somewhere, Jane thought suddenly.

Oh, I must tell Dolly about the bird, and the funeral and all of it, she thought. She'll want to hear all about it.

PART TWO

May - August
1870

⊸⊰ Chapter Nine ⊱⊸

"Look out! Here I come!"

Jane shouted her warning. She gave a mighty push. The tin tea tray on which she was sitting began to slide over the slippery sand. It gained momentum and then suddenly it felt as if she were flying. Wind whistled in her ears as she sped down the steep side of the dune.

She had no control over the tray. It seemed to have a life of its own. Gripping the edges, she felt the rush of air stream over and past her with a glorious sense of speed and space. A fierce, grand exhilaration swelled in her.

The tray hit a tuft of dune grass, lurched, righted itself and flew on down toward the flat beach where Dolly waited.

"Oh, golly!" Jane gasped as she slid to a stop. "That was great!"

Two busy weeks had passed since George Inman's

funeral. The men and boys had helped to pull the wrecked ship off the shoal and to salvage her cargo of lumber. Mama's time had been divided between visits to Mary's cottage and feeding the men, and so Jane had been free to do as she liked.

Today was warm and beautiful, and she had invited Dolly to go sand-sliding, using the big tin trays as sleds.

"Let's have a race," Dolly suggested. "A real race, with bets an' everythin'."

"All right," Jane agreed. "What'll we bet?"

Dolly opened her hand.

She was holding a little ring with a red glass stone, a fairing—the kind of prize given away at fairs.

"I'll wager this ring against your coral beads," she said.

Jane hesitated.

The coral necklace had been a gift from her grandmother. Each bead was cunningly carved in the shape of a tiny chrysanthemum, with a little solid-gold buckle for a clasp. It was one of her most beloved possessions, and worn only on special occasions.

"Well," she said slowly, "I don't know—"

"Oh, come on!" Dolly urged. "Where's your sportin' blood? Don't be a 'fraidy cat!"

That did it. Jane couldn't turn down such a challenge, and she didn't want to face Dolly's scorn.

"All right," she agreed. "It's a deal!"

Slipping and sliding in the dry sand they began to climb the high dune, carrying their tea trays.

"Who'll be the judge?" Jane asked.

"T.J. can do it," Dolly said. "Hey, T.J.—come here."

T. J. took the job seriously. He drew a starting line with his bare toe across the sand at the top of the dune.

"What'll it be?" he asked. "Farthest or fastest?"

"Farthest," Dolly said quickly.

Jane knew that Dolly's greater weight would give her the advantage, but she felt forced to agree.

They sat side by side at the starting line.

"Only fair to push with your hands to start—no feet," T. J. warned. "All right—ready—get set—go!"

Jane leaned forward to give her tray added momentum. She felt rather than saw the dune streak past her. It was so wonderful, like the free, flashing flight of a bird. In the excitement of the ride she completely forgot the race.

Sam chased after them, yelping madly. T. J., sliding in the dry sand, was running after them, shouting, "Come on, Jane! Come on!"

When her tray finally stopped, Jane opened her eyes. There sat Dolly, a good three feet ahead of her on the beach, grinning broadly.

"I won! I won!" she hollered gleefully.

Suddenly Jane thought about her coral beads. A lump formed in her throat and thickened.

"Golly, I don't know," she said as Dolly came up to her. "Mama'll be awful mad. . . ."

Dolly's eyes grew stormy.

"A bet's a bet," she said flatly. "You gotta honor it."

"Well, yes. I know that." Jane's voice was filled with misery. "Will you promise to keep it a secret? I mean, don't wear the beads when Mama's around? 'Cause she doesn't allow us to make bets."

Dolly laughed.

"Oh, sure, if you're so scared. Let's get 'em now."

After the supper dishes were washed that evening, Jane slipped quietly out of the house. She wanted to be by herself for awhile, to think.

The days were getting longer now, and a warm, gold light washed the island from the westering sun. Along the sandy path to the dock on the bay side giant rose mallows nodded gently in the evening wind. They grew nearly as tall as her head.

The soft pink of the great flowers reminded her of her coral necklace. Dolly had dropped it casually into her pocket that afternoon and had gone off laughing.

Jane plucked a flower and tucked it into the bodice of her dress. She was trying to decide what she would tell Mama when the inevitable time would come for an explanation.

As Jane approached the dock where the fishing boats were tied, she saw a solitary figure sitting there looking out across the bay. It was William.

Suddenly she remembered the hidden boat!

In the excitement of the storm and the shipwreck and the funeral she had completely forgotten about it.

She edged down beside William on the rough wooden planking.

"Mind if I sit for awhile?" she asked.

"Be quiet then," he answered. "I'm watching the swans. Look. . . ."

Over across the inlet, at the tip of the next island, a flock of wild swans was floating on the quiet water. They looked like pure, beaten gold in the sunset. Every now and then one of the long sinuous necks would arch and then dip, plunging down into the water. They were foraging among the eel grass in the shallows.

"Golly," Jane said softly. "Aren't they beautiful! William, do you remember that new story Papa read to us last winter? The one by that man who lives in Denmark? What's his name? You know, about the wild swans."

"Hans Christian Andersen," William said. "Yes, I remember."

"I wonder if they are princes in disguise," Jane mused, watching the magnificent stillness of the great birds.

"They're beautiful enough just as they are," William answered. "They don't need to be anything else."

They sat together for awhile, watching the swans in companionable silence. Finally Jane spoke.

"William, I found a boat. Hidden in the cedar swamp."

He turned quickly, his blue eyes narrowing.
"When?"

"Oh, a long time ago—before the wreck."

"Did you say anything to anyone?" he asked.

"No. I saw your secret mark and figured the boat was yours."

He studied her for a long moment.

"Well," he said finally, "I guess you'll have to be in on it."

"I didn't tell—honest! I won't, either. I promise!"

William's eyes were sparkling.

"We want to try for a whale," he said.

"Oh, but—"

He ignored her interruption and went on. "We got

to talking one day—Nat and Harry Lippencott and Ned and Charley Speers and me. Old Captain Cranmer had been telling us about the early days here on the island, when he went whaling from the beach.

"Think of it, Jane! The biggest game in the sea! And it can be done—from a surfboat, I mean. They did it all the time, used to get two or three whales a year. The pods come in close by the island here on their migration—two, three miles out, maybe. Oh, not as many as in the old days, but they still come by."

William looked at her, for she hadn't spoken.

"A pod is what they call a whole bunch of whales. You know, like a school of fish and a flock of birds."

"I know that!" she said impatiently, catching some of his excitement. "Oh, William, do you really think you can do it?"

"I don't know, but we sure can try! We've been practicing with the harpoon. I'm getting pretty good."

He leaned forward in his eagerness to tell her.

"We stuffed some old burlap sacks with dried eel grass. We lay 'em out on the beach, to about the size of a forty-foot whale. And then we practice throwing the harpoon. You've got to know just where to strike —high up, and behind the skull bone, the right place, and the right angle of strike, clean and true."

"T. J. knows about it, doesn't he?"

"Yeah. He caught us one day when we were working on the boat, so we had to tell him. He's our spotter. Being out clamming an' stuff, we don't have much time for whale-watching."

"I sort of figured that," Jane said, "after I found the boat."

"How come you didn't tell?" William asked.

Jane was silent for a moment.

"Oh, I have some secrets too," she said finally.

William made no comment on this. Instead, he went on: "We found this old abandoned surfboat washed up on the beach and fixed it up. Took us about six months. We knew if Papa found out about it he'd say the whole thing was too dangerous. I hate sneaking, honest I do. But if he knew, Papa would never let us try it."

"I know," Jane nodded agreement.

"Jane, just think! If we get one we'll be rich! One —two thousand dollars, maybe! I could go to college without having to borrow the money from Grandfather. I could pay my own way."

"That much money?" Jane breathed in astonishment.

"Yeah—from selling the oil."

"Golly!"

"Of course," he said gloomily, "now it's too late. For this year I mean. Because the whales mostly come in February and March."

"Well, there's next year."

"Yeah, that's true. And there's always an off-chance that there might be one during the summer. Not really likely, but I can still hope."

"William—I'll watch for you too. I'll help T. J."

"Would you?" He smiled at her warmly. "Oh, Jane, you're a brick!"

When Jane went to bed that night she was so busy thinking about whale-watching that she completely forgot about her coral necklace.

-⚜Chapter Ten⚜-

"Jane, I want to talk to you."

Mama was sitting in a rocking chair on the porch shelling beach peas in the warm morning sunlight. Jane, who had been on her way to the rocks with her sketch pad, stopped. Reluctantly she sat down on the porch steps.

Mama looked grave.

"I saw Dolly Speers on the road yesterday. She was wearing the coral necklace that Grandmother gave you."

Jane felt her stomach lurch.

"Would you care to explain?" Mama asked.

"I—I—gave it to her. . . ."

"You *gave* it away?" Mama's voice was shocked.

"Well—I—" Jane floundered. "She—she doesn't have any pretty things, and I—"

"But that necklace is very valuable, Jane. Not just in money—I don't mean that—but in sentiment. A friend of your grandmother's brought it to her from China, on a clipper ship. He was the captain. This was long before she was married. She wore it, and I wore it when I was a girl, and we wanted you to have it, since you're the only grandaughter. It's kind of a family treasure."

Jane hung her head.

"I know, Mama," she mumbled.

"I think it's kind of you to want to share some of your things. I admire you for it. Also, I don't believe in giving a gift and then asking for it back. In this case, however, I think if you were to explain to Dolly, she'd understand. You could give her something to replace it. You could give her your little gold locket, or the shell bracelet. . . ."

"I—I can't do that."

"Why not? The locket's just as pretty, and every bit as valuable in money, if it comes to that."

"Well, Mama—I—it's different. Dolly wants the necklace. You see, I—well, I lost it—the necklace. We had a bet."

"A *bet!*" Mama's eyebrows lifted.

In a rush of misery and a halting voice Jane told her mother about the race. When she had finished, Mama did not speak for a moment. Jane could hear the tiny plonk of peas dropping into the pan. She was afraid to look at her mother's face.

"I see," Mama said finally. "Well, that's that, I guess."

"Oh, Mama. I'm so sorry! I wanted to tell you before, but—"

Mama stood up.

"What's done is done."

Jane waited fearfully for her next words as she turned toward the door.

"I made a custard this morning," Mama said, to Jane's complete astonishment. "I want you to take it over to Mary. You might stop and visit with her for awhile. The poor thing is so lonely."

A few minutes later, as Jane walked over to Mary's cottage carrying the bowl of custard wrapped in a clean towel, she was wondering at Mama's strange reaction. It boded ill, Jane was sure of that, but she couldn't think what her punishment would be.

The cottage door was closed, and when Jane knocked it was a minute or two before Mary answered. Her face wore a slightly guilty look.

"Oh, it's only you, Jane. Come in."

She seemed a bit relieved.

Jane didn't know Mary well. She and George had come to the island during last winter. George was to help Papa and Mr. Lippencott care for the lighthouse. He and Mary had kept to themselves, and Jane had had no opportunity to really get to know her.

Instinctively, however, Jane liked Mary. A tall, big-framed girl, her body now swollen with the expected baby, Mary had a ruddy, open face. Her eyes were the brilliant blue of a summer sea with little laugh crinkles at the corners, and a dash of freckles spattered her nose. She was only eighteen years old.

"My, that looks good," Mary said, peering under the towel at the bowl of custard. "Let's have a dish right now."

"But it's not dinnertime," Jane said in amazement.

"Who's to know?" Mary asked, laughing. "I won't tell if you won't."

She spooned the creamy custard into two bowls and they sat together at the table.

"I'll show you what I was doing when you knocked," Mary said, and then added: "If I looked a little shamefaced, it was only because I thought it might be your mama or Mrs. Lippencott. They'd think I'm too old for such foolishness."

She went to a cupboard and brought a basket back to the table. From it she took some bits of wire, scraps of wadding cotton and little pieces of linen and calico. From the bottom of the basket she carefully lifted a piece of cloth and unwrapped it to reveal two small, wrinkled, human-looking heads.

Jane stared, fascinated.

"I'm making apple dolls," Mary confided.

She handed one of the heads to Jane, who took it gingerly. It was leathery to the touch, and looked exactly like a little old man with a smiling face.

"You peel the apples," Mary explained, "and mark the eyes, nose and mouth with a knife. Then you put them on little sticks and stand them up to dry for about three weeks. You never know quite what they're going to look like."

"They're fascinating!" Jane exclaimed. "They really do look like people! Why this one looks almost like old Captain Cranmer!"

They both giggled.

"Now I'm bending wire to make the bodies," Mary explained. "See—I'll shape it, and then I'll pad it with

cotton and wrap strips of cloth around to make the arms and legs. And then I'll make the clothes."

"Oh, I'd love to try to make one," Jane said enthusiastically. "Of course, I'm too old to play with dolls, but I still like them to look at, you know."

"I've got lots of stuff," Mary said. "Here—I'll show you."

They experimented with bending the wire in various shapes, convulsed with laughter at some of the funny positions they created. As they worked they chattered like two old friends. Jane was amazed how easy it was to talk to Mary. Suddenly she had an idea.

"Why don't we make some little rooms for the dolls to live in?" she suggested. "We could use boxes, like shadow boxes, you know. We could make some tiny furniture, and curtains and rugs. . . ."

Mary clapped her hands together in delight.

"Oh, what a grand idea! You could paint little pictures for the walls, and I'll make some dishes out of shells."

Two hours passed so quickly that Jane could scarcely believe it when she heard the old ship's bell clanging. It hung beside the back door, and Mama used it to call the family to dinner.

"Golly," she cried, leaping up. "I didn't mean to stay so long!"

"I'm glad you did," Mary replied, following her to the door. "I get sort of lonely sometimes. Do come back again soon, won't you?"

"Oh, yes, I really will. I had a wonderful time!"

"And be sure to bring your sketchbook. I want to see your pictures. We'll finish the dolls. I love your idea about making little rooms to mount them in. You can do some sketches and I'll start to make the furniture."

"I'll bring them the next time I come. Bye now!" Jane called, and turned to return Mary's wave as she ran across the dune toward home.

It was after Jane had gone to bed that night that the blow fell.

Half asleep, she heard the knock and Mama opened her bedroom door. She set her lamp on the table and sat down on the bed beside Jane.

"Jane, I think we must talk," Mama began.

Jane scrunched up against the pillow and drew her knees up tight, circling them with her arms.

Here it comes, she thought bitterly.

"Papa and I have been grieved over your behavior lately," Mama said slowly. "Oh, not just one specific thing, but rather a lot of little ones, chores left undone, careless language, rudeness and inattention. But more than anything else, Jane—it's the lying."

Mama folded her hands in her lap and looked at Jane. Jane met her mother's troubled glance and set her mouth in a stubborn line.

"Well, have you anything to say?"

Jane shook her head defiantly.

"All right, then. You've had your chance to speak. Papa and I have decided that a great part of the trouble is Dolly Speers. And so, as your punishment, you will not be allowed to see Dolly again."

Thunderstruck, Jane let out a cry.

"Oh, but, Mama—" she began.

Mama paid no attention to her outburst.

"School is out now for the summer, and there's no reason for Dolly to come up here. Papa will speak to her grandfather and make our position clear."

"But—she's my friend," Jane protested.

If she'd had any doubts about her feelings for Dolly they were now swept away by her resentment at Mama's unfairness.

"She's not your true friend," Mama replied. "She cheated you out of your grandmother's necklace."

"She didn't cheat!" Jane flared. "She won it fair and square."

"She may have won it, but to ask you to wager it in the first place was wrong."

Although Jane argued stormily, Mama would not relent. She finally left the room, her starched petticoats rustling.

After Mama had gone, Jane buried her face in the pillow and wept bitter tears.

It's not fair, she thought angrily, it's just not fair! And I don't care what she says—Dolly *is* my friend! Even if I'm never allowed to see her again, she's still my very best friend.

She pulled the quilt over her head to muffle the sound of her sobbing.

I think I'll run away, she thought.

That's what I'll do. I'll just run away!

-◄Chapter Eleven►-

On her way downstairs the next morning Jane decided that she would spend the day on whale-watch. She wanted to be alone to think, and she didn't feel like having to make conversation with any of the family.

William had nailed several boards to the top of the old pine tree by T. J.'s shanty, making a tiny platform. Jane had discovered that if she was careful how she folded her legs she could sit up there quite comfortably.

She'd begun a drawing of a pine bough she could see from this perch, a cluster of tiny cones, and each separate needle with a furry tuft at its base. She could finish the drawing, and be alone to sort out her thoughts.

Today was T. J.'s day to watch, but Jane knew he'd

be delighted to be free. He was already at the table stuffing himself with muffins. Butter ran in a yellow rivulet down his chin.

Mama was not there, but Jane lowered her voice anyway.

"I'll take the watch today," she whispered.

"Anachronistic!" he exclaimed. "I wanted to go swimmin', anyway."

Jane poured a tumbler of milk for herself and buttered a muffin.

"I really don't think the whales are goin' to come this year," T. J. said, brushing crumbs from his shirtfront. "I seen six ships go by yesterday, but nothin' else."

"Saw," Jane corrected his grammer automatically. "I 'spose not. But William'd have a fit if they did come, and we missed them."

Just then the kitchen door flew open and Mama rushed in, her hair windtorn and her face worried.

"Where's William?" she demanded.

"He's not up yet," T. J. replied.

Mama was already in the hall, calling up the stairs.

"William! William! Hurry and get up! I want you to sail over to the mainland and fetch Dr. DiGiovanni."

Jane glanced anxiously at her mother when she returned to the kitchen.

"Has there been an accident, Mama? Is someone hurt?"

"No, child. It's Mary. Her baby will be born today."

"Hey, anachronistic!" T. J. whistled. "Can we watch?"

Last year he and Jane had watched a litter of kittens being born.

81

"Of course not!" Mama snapped. "Now, T. J.—you just go out and play. And try to keep out of trouble!"

She turned to Jane.

"I want you to prepare dinner for the family, and make the beds and don't forget to feed the chickens."

Mama was gathering together some kettles and a pile of clean white linen towels, talking over her shoulder as she spoke.

"Mind now, you make a good dinner. Fry that catch of fish William brought in last night. And don't forget vegetables. And there's a prune cake for dessert."

Mama was already on her way out the door.

"I'm going to stay with Mary. And Jane, don't you come bothering down to the cottage. You just handle things here by yourself."

She was gone.

William appeared a few minutes later, rubbing his eyes sleepily, his hair tousled.

"Darn it," he said, "I had plans for today. Oh, well. Will you fix me something, Jane? I'll eat it on the way over."

Jane found herself with so much work to do that day that the hours flew by. About eleven o'clock, from an upstairs window as she was making beds, she saw William's boat come tacking down the bay. As it slid into the dock, the doctor leaped ashore, carrying his black leather bag.

All the children adored Dr. DiGiovanni. He was a short, stocky young man with a crest of shining black hair and a profile Papa said came straight from a Roman coin. His speaking voice was husky, tinged with a trace of his native Calabria, and his singing was a pure miracle—a deep, strong basso.

On every visit to the island he always took time to entertain the family with arias from *La Traviata*, *Aida* and *Il Trovatore*. He also loved the folk songs of his adopted land with a passion. Jane felt shivers of delight every time he sang the rollicking sea chanteys, or the haunting notes of her favorite, "Shenandoah." She wished that he lived on the island and could spend more time with them.

From time to time during the day Jane looked over toward the cottage, but there was no sign of any activity save for a thread of smoke drifting above the chimney.

Part of her was curious to know exactly what was going on, and the other part of her was glad not to be there. She knew a little about babies and how they got born, not from Mama, but from old Mrs. Cranmer. And Jane had decided she wasn't ever going to have a baby.

Papa was on first watch that night, so Jane fixed supper early. He had already gone to the lighthouse before the sun had set, and Jane had nearly finished washing the dishes when Mama walked into the kitchen. Her face looked tired but she was smiling. She caught Jane to her in a close embrace.

"It's a boy," she said, "a lovely baby boy."

"Oh, how wonderful!" Jane cried, surprised at Mama's warmth.

"Would you like to see him?"

"Oh, yes! May I—really?"

"Yes, you run along over. Just don't stay too long. Only a few minutes."

Jane stopped on the porch of the big house long enough to pick up the bouquet of flowers she had gathered that afternoon. They were Mary's favorites—the delicate, frothy Queen Anne's lace, and creamy yarrow with its fernlike leaves, and starred within were little gold buttons of dandelion blossoms and rich purple fronds of flowering vetch. She had arranged them in a gray stone crock, and tucked in among the leaves was a tiny picture of a baby she had drawn.

As Jane cautiously opened the cottage door, not knowing quite what to expect, the first sound she heard coming from the open door of the bedroom was singing!

> Hush little baby, don't say a word,
> Mama's goin' to buy you a mockin' bird,
> An' if that mockin' bird don't sing,
> Mama's goin' to buy you a diamond ring . . .

The doctor's deep voice, slurred now and soft, was crooning a lullaby.

Dr. DiGiovanni was sitting in a rocking chair by the window holding a tiny bundle wrapped in a soft woolen blanket. Mary lay on the bed, her face pale but shining as if lit from inside by a candle.

"Ah, leetle Zhanie!" the doctor cried softly. "Come een, come een."

"Oh, Jane," Mary said, her voice weak, but her face breaking into a smile, "I'm so glad you came! Come—see the baby."

Jane bent and looked into the little face as Dr. DiGiovanni pulled back the blanket. It was so funny, screwed up and red and wrinkled, just like one of the apple dolls.

"Isn't he beautiful?" Mary said, her eyes shining.

Jane swallowed hard.

"Oh—yes—" she lied valiantly. "Why, he's just —well, he's really—quite a baby!"

"His name is George," Mary said proudly. "George Andrew Inman, after his papa."

"He looks pretty little for such a big name," Jane observed.

The doctor threw back his head and laughed heartily.

"Thees fellow weel grow into eet pretty fast," he said.

Before she left, Jane was allowed to hold the tiny bundle. She was afraid she might drop the baby, and sat very stiff. He stirred slightly in her arms and blinked his milky little eyes but he didn't cry.

Jane looked up at Mary and the doctor with a wide smile.

"Say—he really is kind of nice, isn't he?" she said in amazement.

The next morning after she had finished her chores, Jane collected her sketch pad and pencils and slipped quietly out of the house. She headed for her rock cave on the beach. As she clambered across the top she noticed a flash of red.

Dolly was sitting in the little cave, her back leaning against one of the rocks.

"Cripes!" she said when she saw Jane, "I thought you'd never come! I been waitin' for two days."

Jane dropped down to the soft sand.

"Oh, Dolly!" she cried. "I'm so glad to see you. I never thought you'd come to the cave."

Then suddenly she felt embarrassed.

"We're not supposed to see each other—" she began.

"Yeah, I know," Dolly said. "Gran'pap tole me."

"I'm so mad at Mama!" Jane said angrily.

"She sure is a mean one," Dolly agreed. "But I figger, what she don't know won't hurt 'er."

Jane told Dolly about Mary's baby being born, and they discussed this for awhile. And then they began to talk about the long summer stretching ahead of them.

"Mama just doesn't understand how it is with me," Jane complained. "She and Papa have each other. It's kind of like—well, like I'm in the way all the time. T. J. has Sam, and William has lots of friends, and for me there's just no one—till you came, that is."

"Grown-ups are always like that," Dolly observed. "They just think that all young folks are good for is for bossin' around and workin'."

"But your grandfather isn't like that—he doesn't boss you around."

"Nope," Dolly agreed, and then added shrewdly, "but that's only because he don't care about me, not really. All he cares about is drinkin'."

They sat together in silence.

"I was thinking about running away," Jane said suddenly.

Dolly sat up. Her eyes glittered.

"No foolin'? You mean it?"

"Yes, I really was."

"That'd fix 'er—your ma! Whyn't we go together?"

"Well," Jane said slowly, "It's just that I—I don't know where to go. I mean, where can you run away to when you live on a little island?"

86

"We can think o' someplace," Dolly said.

She leaped to her feet and began to pace restlessly.

"Yeah," she said. "Why not? Let's do it, Jane! We can figger it all out first—how we're goin' to do it, an' where we're goin' an' all. I'm bustin' to get off this dumb old island, anyway."

Dolly turned to Jane, her face glowing.

"Why, yeah! We could find ourselves some work —like hired girls, maybe. Just till we get ourselves enough money to git to Philadelphia or Richmond."

Jane began to catch some of her excitement.

"Oh, Dolly! We could, couldn't we? If we were together it'd be all right. I mean, I wouldn't be so scared then. I'll bet there are a lot of farms over on the mainland where they'd hire us. We could earn some money, and. . . ."

"Tell you what," Dolly said. "This'll take some plannin'. We got to be cagey, you know, so's no one'll know where we got to, an' can come after us. We'll think on it some, and meet here again tomorrow mornin'."

"You're right," Jane agreed. "It'd never do to let on. We've go to do it in secret."

A thought crossed her mind.

"Not that Mama'd even care," she added grimly. "She'll probably be glad to get rid of me. I'm nothing but trouble to her. Maybe she'll be sorry then. . . ."

-*Chapter Twelve*-

Dolly again was waiting for her when Jane arrived at the rocks the next morning. She had told Mama she was going to visit Mary, and had indeed paid a quick call at the cottage. So it's not a real lie, she thought as she clambered over the rocks.

Dolly's face was flushed with excitement and the heat of the day.

"Look," she began without preamble. "I got an idea. You got any money?"

"I have three silver dollars," Jane replied. "Grandfather always gives me one for my birthday and at Christmas."

"Is that all? I don't reckon that's enough," Dolly said, disappointed. "I was thinkin', see, if we could get across the bay to Tuckerton, we could get the stagecoach for Philadelphia. But that'd take money—for fares. I'm certain sure we could get us work in a big place like Philadelphia, an' somethin' that'd be better than a hired girl on a farm. Why, we might even get us a job in a store, or somethin'."

Jane pondered this alluring prospect.

"How much money do you think it'd take?" she asked.

"I don't rightly know, but I'll ask around. Surely your Pa's got some money."

"Yes, but I couldn't ask him. He'd want to know why."

"'Course you can't *ask* him! Don't be so dumb! Just lift it when he's not lookin'."

"Oh . . . but that would be stealing!"

"Can you think of any other way?"

Jane was silent.

"Well—no—I guess not," she said finally, and then she added, "I've got a birthday in three weeks, and I'll probably get another dollar. . . ."

Dolly shook her head.

"That won't be enough. I know where gran'pap hides his cash, but there ain't nothin' there. I looked. I'll keep a sharp watch, though. No sense in startin' out without enough money to see us through for awhile," she said practically.

They talked further, discussing ways of getting to Tuckerton, a town farther south on the mainland. The stage from Philadelphia stopped there, and the people who came to Long Beach Island for a summer vacation got boats at Tuckerton to sail them across the bay.

The beautiful summer weather was holding, and the

day was hot and bright. Jane was wearing a swimming costume Mama had made for her from dark blue flannel. It had a high neck, long drawers that reached her ankles and sleeves that came to her wrists.

"Come on," she said to Dolly finally. "I'm dying with the heat! Let's go swimming."

She knew that the beach beyond the rocks was well out of sight of the big house, and Mama wouldn't see them.

"I can't swim," Dolly protested.

"I'll show you. It's easy," Jane said. "And besides, it's low tide now. We can walk way out to the sandbar. See—where the waves are breaking out there? It'll cool us off."

Dolly stripped off her tattered skirt and her shoes, and gingerly waded into the surf after Jane.

"Cripes!" she said. "This petticoat weighs a ton when it's wet. Wait a minute."

Deftly she pulled it up and tied it between her legs.

"There now. That's better!"

She looked at Jane in her long flannel swimming suit.

"You look kinda crazy," she laughed.

"At least I don't have to wear a hat and a skirt, like the ladies from Philadelphia," Jane replied defensively.

The water was deliciously cool. They splashed knee deep for a hundred yards and reached the sandbar, where little waves were breaking playfully. Jane flopped on her stomach in the shallow water and let the white bubbly foam wash over her.

"Isn't this heavenly?" she cried, rolling on her back and splashing with her arms.

Sun sparkled on the gentle summer waves as they broke, sending speckles of white foam swirling. It seemed as if the whole world was flashing signals of white and blue and gold.

The sky arched high, and the water rushed and danced with its sweet sting of salt spray. Nothing was important but this blissful moment. Jane felt as if she were a glorious part of bubbling white water and blue sky, as if there had never been anything before, and would never be anything again save this miracle.

They laughed and splashed each other and romped through the water for nearly an hour. It was only slowly that Jane realized that the tide had turned and was beginning to come in. Already water that had been ankle deep on the sandbar was now knee deep. Jane knew that they had to cross a trough between the sandbar and the beach, and Dolly couldn't swim!

The trough was only about twenty feet wide, and they had walked across it easily earlier at low tide. But now the water was deepening rapidly. Jane knew she could swim it with no trouble, but she doubted that she could carry Dolly.

Dolly was still rolling and laughing in the fizzy surf, splashing and shouting. Jane felt a moment of panic. She didn't want to frighten her friend.

And then she remembered the old breeches buoy T.J. kept in his shanty.

"Hey, I've got an idea," she called to Dolly, trying to keep her voice deceptively calm. "You wait here for a few minutes and I'll be right back."

She started across the trough and found as she had suspected that the water was already over her head in depth.

"You stay there," she called back to Dolly. "Don't move and stay right on the sandbar till I get back."

Dolly was enjoying herself and didn't seem at all concerned. Jane began to swim as Papa had taught her, with strong, even strokes.

Panting, she finally reached the beach and began to run toward the shanty, which was quite some distance away. As she ran she prayed that the breeches buoy would still be there. It was an old one, discarded by the life-saving crew, and Papa had given it to her and T. J. to use as a plaything.

The breeches buoy was a round, cork-filled ring, like a huge doughnut, fitted with a pair of rough canvas pants with short legs. When a rope was fastened to it, and then to a pulley on the lifeline, a person could be hauled in comparative safety across a stormy sea from a sinking ship to land.

Jane breathed a sigh of relief when she found the old buoy, covered with cobwebs, in a corner of the shanty. She snatched it up and ran back as fast as she could.

By now the water in the trough was deep, and Jane, carrying the bulky buoy, began to swim across to the sandbar. Dolly, now waist deep in water, stood watching her with anxious eyes.

"Hey, I was gettin' scared! What you got there?" she called as Jane approached her.

"It's an old breeches buoy." Jane was gasping for breath. "Here—put it on—you put your feet through these holes. . . ."

In the tumbling waves it was hard to stand up, but she finally managed to get Dolly into the contraption.

"Are you sure this'll work?" Dolly asked nervously.

"Yes," Jane assured her. "Now we've got to get back to the beach as fast as we can, 'cause the tide's coming in. You kick with your feet and I'll swim beside you and push. Ready?"

With Dolly kicking frantically and bobbing about in the buoy, and Jane swimming and pushing, they finally reached the safety of shallow water. They crawled up onto the warm sand and stretched out.

"Cripes! Am I tired!" Jane sighed.

Dolly eyed her crossly.

"I might 'a drownded out there!" she said.

Jane looked at her through a film of exhaustion, too tired to speak.

"You said it was easy. You might-a got me killed."

"I'm sorry, Dolly. Truly, I am."

"Well, all right. But I'm not doin' any more swimmin', so jest don't ask me."

They lay quietly for awhile, soaking up the delicious warmth of the sun. Suddenly Dolly broke the silence,

"There's goin' to be a dance at the Harvey Cedars Hotel next Saturday night. Let's go, Jane."

"I'd never be allowed," Jane said, rolling lazily over onto her stomach.

"You could slip off. No one'd know. There's goin' to be three fiddlers, an' it'll be a grand time. Come on—we'll have a pack o' fun!"

"I've never been to a dance before," Jane replied, sifting sand through her fingers. "In fact, I don't even know how to dance."

"It's easy. Your partner leads you around. An' anyway, we can jest watch. A lot o' summer folks'll be there, so there wouldn't be no one to snitch on you."

"I'd love to go," Jane said wistfully.

She thought of the past week, and how she'd helped preserve about a bushel of huckleberries, and of how she'd cleaned the henhouse and swept the rugs. She was sure there was such a thing as too much virtue. Then too, it would make up to Dolly for getting her into danger this afternoon.

And anyway, she didn't much care if she did get caught. She wasn't going to be around much longer, if the plan worked.

"All right," she said, "I'll do it! I'll come!"

--⊰ Chapter Thirteen ⊱--

As Jane drew near the big cedar-shingled Harvey Cedars Hotel on Saturday night, she could hear the scrape of fiddles from some distance away. At the hitching rail a few horses were tied, and several wagons stood about the yard. As she approached, Dolly stepped out from the shadow of one of them.

Jane was astonished at the change in her friend. Dolly was wearing a blue silk dress with little velvet ribbons at the throat and a deep ruffle on the skirt. Only when she looked closely did she notice that the silk was slit in several places and the ribbons were faded. Dolly's dark hair was a mass of curly ringlets.

"Cripes!" Jane exclaimed. "You look marvelous!"

She was wearing her second-best sprigged lawn dress with its little-girl sash.

"Oh, it's an old one of my mam's—one she left behind," Dolly said airly. "But I put my hair up in curl-papers. How does it look?"

She twirled around.

"Just beautiful!" Jane replied admiringly, and a little enviously.

"I was afraid you was goin' to back out," Dolly said.

"I said I'd come, didn't I?"

Jane was nervous. She didn't really want to be here, and she didn't know how to act. Suddenly she felt a little resentful toward Dolly for getting her into this.

"There's lots o' fellas," Dolly whispered, taking her arm and leading her up the steps to the wide veranda.

Jane made no reply, but allowed herself to be led, her heart fluttering in her chest.

In the big bare dining room of the hotel the tables had been pushed back against the walls. Three men stood on one of the tables sawing energetically at their fiddles, and a heavy man with a red beard stood in front of them, stamping his foot and singing.

> Come all ye young fellows that follow the sea,
> To my way, haye, blow the man down,
> And pay, pay attention and listen to me,
> Give me some time to blow the man down . . .

A group of men, their arms entwined, were dancing in a circle to the tune of the old sea chantey. Around the edge of the room young girls and older women were clapping their hands in time to the music.

Jane, standing in the doorway with Dolly, scanned the room hastily to see if there was anyone she knew. But everyone seemed to be a stranger, and she breathed a little easier.

These were all summer people who came from Philadelphia to take the sea air. They considered it a lark to rough it in the crude local accommodations, to go boating and fishing and clamming in the bay and to bathe in the surf.

The fiddles stopped and the red-bearded man wiped his jovial sweating face with a large handkerchief.

"Now for a reel," he called. "Ladies and gentlemen—take your places! Gents, choose yourself a lovely little lady, an' line 'er up!"

A tall boy with an impudent smiling face approached Jane and Dolly. Jane found herself shrinking back, but she needn't have worried, for the boy didn't even glance at her.

"Come on, sweetheart," he said to Dolly. "Let's have a fling!"

"Oooo! I'd like that!" Dolly giggled.

Without a backward glance, Dolly stepped out onto the floor with the boy. Jane found herself standing alone.

The reel began, and she watched fascinated as the dancers whirled around to the lively music. Each time Dolly passed near her, Jane could see her smiling up at the boy, her blue skirt ruffle swirling up and out.

After two more dances Jane began to get bored. No one paid the least attention to her. There was a big punch bowl set up on a table at the back of the room, and Jane noticed people going over to it and helping themselves from time to time.

Her mouth felt dry, so she edged her way around the room to the table and filled a tumbler for herself from the big bowl. It looked like cider, but it tasted quite different. It was delicious, and Jane drank thirstily.

"Hey, little girl! What are you doing?"

A tall man with kindly smile-crinkled eyes was looking down at her.

Jane blushed.

"I—I was thirsty," she murmured.

Gently he bent down and took the nearly empty tumbler from her hand.

"Well, my dear, I don't think you should be drinking this. You wait here, and I'll get you some lemonade."

He disappeared into the crowd.

Jane was so embarrassed she wanted to die. Desperately she began to search for Dolly. Finally she saw her, sitting on the edge of a table in the corner talking with her dancing partner. Jane made her way over quickly, before the tall man would return.

In her haste, she interrupted rudely.

"I'm going home," she said to Dolly.

Dolly just looked at her in surprise.

"Why? Just when the fun's startin'!"

"Well—I just have to go now," Jane replied stubbornly. "So come on. . . ."

"Suit yourself," Dolly replied with a shrug, "I'm stayin'."

She turned back to the boy, ignoring Jane.

Jane hesitated for a moment, her face burning. Then she turned away quickly and ran from the room, pushing her way blindly through the growing crowd of people. She pelted headlong across the veranda and down the steps.

Hot tears of humiliation drenched her cheeks as she hurried down the road toward home. Her side hurt from running, and she began to hiccup.

Finally she slowed down when the now-hateful sound of the fiddle music was only a whisper. It was very dark and quiet, the deep sky spattered with stars and far off, the hushed murmuring of the surf on the shore.

Jane felt dizzy and sick. She dragged herself to a clump of bayberry bushes at the side of the path and threw up. She knelt there in the sand, her head in her hands.

At last, feeling weak but much better, she slowly rose and began walking toward home. As she approached she could hear voices from the front porch of the big house where Mama and Mrs. Lippencott were sitting. Quietly she slipped in through the kitchen door and went up to her room.

Without bothering to undress, Jane flung herself down on her bed. Sobs of anger and humiliation racked her small frame. She muffled her face in the pillow.

Oh, I hate her! I hate her! she thought bitterly. How could she be so cruel? She's supposed to be my friend!

I hate everybody!

Nobody cares about *me*—just nobody!

After a long while she got up and slowly poured water from the big pitcher into her washbowl. It felt cool and sweet on her flushed face.

Well, I'll show them, she thought grimly. I'll just show *all* of them. . . .

PART THREE

September - October
1870

--⚜Chapter Fourteen ⚜--

"Open your mouth," Mama commanded.

Jane clenched her teeth tightly and shook her head.

Mama was holding a spoonful of the dreadful Tonispah tonic.

"Jane Sibylla! Don't you dare defy me! Now you just
take this! You've been moping around for two weeks
now."

"Oh, Mama—just let me alone!" Jane cried in desperation.

She pushed past her mother and ran to the kitchen
door. The thick black tonic spilled from the spoon
down the front of her mother's clean apron.

Mama gazed after her in astonishment.

"Jane! You come back here this minute. . . ."

But Jane was already out the door and running
across the dune. Tears streamed down her cheeks.

When she reached the solitude of the beach she flung herself down on the sand, sobbing bitterly. She was just one great tangled knot of misery.

Things had been going from bad to worse ever since the night of the dance. For two weeks now Jane had moped and sulked, inwardly raging.

She had refused to go down to the rocks for any secret meetings with Dolly. She didn't care if she ever saw her again. To make matters worse, school was to start tomorrow. Jane wondered if Dolly would come, and if she did, how would things be between them.

She had been doing a lot of thinking, and she was sure now that she didn't want to run away with Dolly. Jane wondered if she had enough courage to go by herself. She had made a dozen plans in the last two weeks, and each time had abandoned them.

The final straw was that William had left yesterday for college. The house felt so lonely without him. The night before he left Jane had had a few minutes to talk with him privately.

"I'm so sorry that the whales didn't come," Jane told him.

"Well, that's the way things are sometimes," William replied philosophically.

"You want us to keep watching anyway?"

"Hardly seems worthwhile now," William answered. "I'm not bragging, mind, but it's just that I don't think the other boys could handle it by themselves. Tell you what, though. I'd sure appreciate it if you'd keep an eye on the boat. We've got a lot of time and work invested in that. Not that anyone's likely to find it, but I'd really catch it from Papa if it was discovered."

"I'll see it stays hidden," Jane promised, and then added: "You can count on me!"

Impulsively she hugged her brother.

"Oh, William—I'm going to miss you something awful!"

"Well, I'll be home for Christmas," he said cheerfully. "And, Jane—I'll send you that new sketchbook you need."

With William gone everything seemed to be falling apart all at once. Jane had never openly defied her mother before, but she just didn't care.

Finally her tears stopped. She felt drained and exhausted. The day stretched drearily ahead of her, and she sat up staring moodily out across the wrinkling sea. Kelp was drifting in dark ribbons just beneath the surface, shifting with the current as sinuous as a sea serpent.

"Jane . . . . Oh, Jane!"

Hearing her name called, she looked up.

Mary was coming across the dunes, carrying baby Georgie Indian fashion in a kind of sling fashioned from a strip of blanket.

"I've been looking for you," Mary said, coming up to her and sitting down beside her on the sand.

She shifted the baby onto her lap.

"I've missed you," Mary said. "I've been so busy with the baby and all. But I do hope we can get back to finishing our apple dolls."

Jane felt a little pang of guilt. She had been so busy with her own problems she had nearly forgotten about the dolls.

"I—I guess I should have come over, but I thought—maybe you didn't want to bother. . . ."

"Bother!" Mary laughed. "Why, knowing you has been just about the nicest thing that's happened to me lately . . . . next to this little fellow."

She looked tenderly at the baby on her lap. He waved his pudgy little fists.

Jane felt a slow surprise fill her.

"You really mean that?" she asked.

"Of course I do! I can talk to you like—well, it's different than with older folks. It's hard to explain."

Jane nodded.

I know what you mean, she thought. She suddenly felt an urge to tell Mary about her own problems. But before she could speak, Mary broke the silence.

"Jane, can I tell you a secret? I've—I've just got to talk to someone."

Jane pulled her attention reluctantly back from her own thoughts. Mary's face was somber, and she was staring out to sea.

"I think maybe the doctor wants to marry me," she said abruptly.

Jane's eyes widened in surprise.

"Oh, Mary! Has he asked you?"

"Well, no. Not really, that is. But I have a feeling he's going to. . . ."

"Well, my gosh!" Jane said. "He's so—old! Do you like him?"

Mary considered this before answering.

"Y-yes, I really do like him. Oh, I don't love him —like George, I mean. But he's kind and gentle and good."

Jane scratched her head.

"Come to think of it, I did notice that he's been

coming over to the island nearly every day. But I didn't realize. . . ."

Mary smiled.

"He says it's to check on the baby, but the baby's fine. He says he likes my clam fritters too. He says he gets pretty lonely living all by himself and eating his own cooking."

She was silent for a moment and then went on.

"I'll be truthful with you, Jane. I really do need someone to look after baby Georgie and me. You see, we don't have any money left at all. Your Papa and Mr. Lippencott have been so kind, letting us stay on at the cottage and all, but I can't go on like this much longer. When the baby's older maybe I can get a job somewhere, but he's still too little, and I—I just don't know what to do. . . ."

Jane saw there were tears glistening in Mary's eyes. Impulsively she took her hand and squeezed it.

"Oh, Mary, things will work out for you. I just know it! And you know, Dr. DiGiovanni is really an awfully nice man. I mean, he's so handsome, and he can sing and—"

Mary dried her eyes on her sleeve.

"I know I'm being foolish. It's just that I do miss George so much! I try to be brave, but—"

Suddenly Jane really saw Mary for the very first time. She felt a quick surge of admiration.

"Oh, you are brave! Why, you're just about the bravest person I've ever met. I mean it!"

Mary gave her a wan smile.

"Thanks, Jane. Just being able to talk to someone helps so much!"

-•≪ Chapter Fifteen ≫•-

Jane found that she couldn't sleep that night. She had so much to think about that her mind felt like a Fourth of July Catherine wheel, fizzing and spinning. Finally, after tossing about for what seemed like hours, she decided to go down to the kitchen for a glass of water.

The door to the hallway was closed, and Jane was just about to push it open when she noticed a sliver of light beneath, and heard voices. Papa and Mama must be sitting at the kitchen table drinking tea, she thought.

Jane didn't mean to eavesdrop, but she couldn't help herself when a name caught her ear. She leaned furtively against the closed door.

"—it's perfectly ridiculous!" Mama was saying. "Dr. DiGiovanni is old enough to be her father!"

"Now, Martha"—Papa's gentle voice was reproachful—"he's only twenty-eight."

"Well, I think we ought to speak to Mary."

"Martha! You don't even know if he's asked her."

"He wouldn't be traipsing over here to the island every day if something wasn't afoot."

"If he loves Mary, he'd make her a fine husband," Papa said. "He's fond of the baby, and I know he'd be good to both of them. But what's important above all, Martha, is that it's none of our business! Mary is old enough to make her own decisions. You mean well, my dear, but you can't live everyone's life for them."

"Well, I think it's just ... foolishness! Why, he's even *shorter* than she is!"

Papa's rich, soft laughter filled the room.

"Oh, Martha! That's the limit! What a qualification for marriage! Is that why you married me? Because I'm taller than you are?"

Mama began to laugh, too.

"Silly!" she cried softly. "You know I married you because you're the handsomest, kindest, most intelligent man in the whole world!"

"Careful now, Martha—you just might be having me believe that. . . ."

There was a long silence, and then Jane heard Mama's voice, low and trembling.

"Oh, dearest, I just hate myself sometimes! I get so quick and cross with all of you. You're right, you know. I *am* bossy, and I don't mean to be. I get provoked, and then I say and do things I'm sorry for —especially with Jane. I don't know what's wrong with me!"

109

"There's nothing wrong with you, my dear." Papa's voice was gentle. "I know how lonely it is for you here on the island, with your family and friends so far away."

"But *you* are my family, you and the children."

"I know that, but . . . . Look here, I have a wonderful idea! Sometime soon we'll take a little excursion, just the two of us. I hear there's a new wooden street just been built in Atlantic City. They call it a boardwalk. It runs right along the beach. We'll go and take a look at it together, and I'll treat you to an elegant supper at the Surf House."

"Oh, Will! But we ought to take the children too. They'd enjoy it so much."

"Not this time," Papa said firmly. "Just the two of us."

"Oh, that would be lovely."

Jane turned and slowly crept back upstairs, feeling more lonely and shut-out than ever.

Dolly did not appear for lessons the next morning. Mama made no comment on this, but calmly went about giving assignments. Jane found her attention wandering, but Mama seemed to be pointedly ignoring her and she was grateful at least for that.

As the week went by and still Dolly did not come to school, Jane began to feel uneasy. She was in the curious position of not wanting to see her, and yet wondering where she was and what she was doing.

So every afternoon Jane went down to the rocks and waited, hoping Dolly might appear. But Dolly never came.

It was Friday before her patience was finally rewarded. Dolly was waiting for her. It was an awkward moment for Jane, but Dolly seemed unperturbed. She jumped to her feet when she saw Jane.

"I got big news," she announced without even first saying hello. "Guess what? I'm gettin' married!"

Jane gaped in astonishment.

"You're *what?*"

"You surprised, huh?" Dolly laughed. "Me too, kinda! 'Member the fella I met at the dance? His name's Frank. Well, I was tellin' him 'bout us plannin' to run away, an' he says why not come along with him?"

"But Dolly—you hardly know him!"

Dolly winked broadly.

"Oh, I've got to know him all right, these past few days! He's a right enough fella, an' he's rich—his pap's got a lot 'o money."

"But Dolly—you're only fifteen!"

"Oh, pooh! Lottsa girls get married at fifteen."

Jane was at a complete loss for words.

Dolly tossed her head.

"So—I come to say good-bye."

"But Dolly! What about us? I thought we were going together?"

Jane forgot all about her earlier decision.

Dolly looked at her coolly.

"I thought maybe you didn't want to do it anymore. After you run off an' left me at the dance, an' all. Well, I spose you could come along, part of the ways, anyway. . . ."

She considered this for a moment.

"Yeah, why not? I'll tell Frank. He's got plans for us to get to Tuckerton tomorrow night, an' then seats on the stage for the next mornin'. No reason why you couldn't come that far with us. Tell you what—I'll go see Frank, an' meet you here tomorrow, an' let you know for sure."

Dolly clambered up over the rocks.

"I got to go now," she said. "See you. . . ."

And she was gone, running over the dune, her red shawl streaming in the wind.

Jane stared after her, stunned.

Chapter Sixteen

The next morning as Jane started out to meet Dolly she knew exactly what she was going to do. Instead of going down to the rocks she walked boldly down the road.

For the first time in many weeks her mind was perfectly clear and firm, on one point at least. It was a good feeling, to have made a decision and to know that she had the strength to stand by it.

Jane had gone scarcely a mile when she saw Dolly coming, and she began to run toward her.

Before Dolly could speak Jane called out.

"I'm not coming with you."

Dolly looked startled.

"But Frank said—"

"I don't care what he said," Jane plunged ahead, "and another thing: Dolly, I don't think you ought to go either—not with Frank, anyway."

Dolly planted her feet firmly on the road and put her hands on her hips. She stared belligerently at Jane.

"You're just jealous, that's what!"

"No, I'm not," Jane replied calmly, returning her stare. "Oh, maybe I was, a little, just at first. But I've been doing a lot of thinking. Dolly, I don't think Frank is going to marry you, and I think you'll just get yourself into a lot of trouble."

She looked at her friend with concern.

"Please. Don't go."

Dolly tossed her head.

"A fat lot you know! He's crazy about me. You're just a—little kid! And a scaredy-cat, that's what!"

And with that she turned on her heel and walked away.

Jane felt tears sting her eyes. But curiously it was not because of Dolly's scornful words. Jane ran after her.

"Dolly—listen, please! I'll go with you, like we planned, honest I will. But not with Frank—that's what's all wrong."

Dolly did not stop or even turn her head.

"You just go on back home to your mama," she said. "We didn't want you anyway. Now—just leave me alone!"

She began to run.

Jane watched her sadly for a few minutes. Then she slowly turned around and walked home.

As Jane came up to the big house she saw that Mama was standing on the porch, drawing on her gloves. A suitcase stood by the door. Mama's face looked strained and pale.

"I'm glad you got back before I left," she said stiffly as Jane came up the steps. "I'm going to Philadelphia for a few days to visit your grandparents. You'll have to keep house for Papa and T. J. while I'm gone."

Papa came out the door just then and picked up the suitcase.

"Janie, I'm going to take Mama over to Tuckerton to get the stage," he said. "You take good care of T. J. till I get home."

With mixed feelings of bewilderment and a queer kind of relief, Jane stood rigid as Mama bent and kissed her on the cheek. Without any further word of explanation, Mama started toward the dock where the skiff was moored. She did not turn to wave.

Jane watched as the little boat slid away from the dock and then she turned and slowly walked into the house. It was puzzling, Mama going off so suddenly like this, but Jane felt sure Papa would explain it to her when he returned.

As she entered the kitchen, so big and quiet, she didn't know why, but suddenly she felt happy! She flung out her arms and slowly swung about.

Oh, how wonderful, she thought, to have the whole house to myself! I hope Mama stays away a long, long time!

When Papa arrived home late in the afternoon, the table was neatly set and a pan of fish was crackling on the stove. A fresh buttercake on Mama's best cut-glass cake stand stood on the center of the table, and her Parian vase in the shape of a hand was filled with sprays of goldenrod and Queen Anne's lace.

T. J., who had grumbled some, was wearing a clean shirt, and his unruly mop of hair was neatly brushed.

115

Papa was clearly impressed.

"Why Janie!" he exclaimed. "How pretty everything looks! And you baked a cake, too. It looks delicious!"

He praised the dinner, and even T. J. grudgingly admitted it was "pretty anachronistic." Jane wanted to ask why Mama had suddenly decided to go to Philadelphia, but Papa didn't seem inclined to talk and so she decided to let well enough alone.

Her pride of accomplishment was enough for now. It was a marvelous feeling to be in charge of the house and to be doing it well.

After supper she carefully washed the dishes and mixed up a batch of bread dough, covering it carefully with a piece of flannel and setting it to rise on top of the still warm stove.

At bedtime she saw T. J. safely tucked in and heard his prayers and finally went to bed herself, worn out but well satisfied with her day.

In the morning Jane couldn't find Mama's recipe for griddle cake batter, so she sort of made up one. They were a little heavy, but not too bad. Papa took a final swallow of his coffee and leaned back in his chair.

"Looks like the three of us will have to hold the fort around here today," he remarked. "The bluefish came in last night, a good run of them this year by the looks of it. All of the men went out early."

He walked over to the window where sunlight glinted like tiny fire opals on the glass.

"A fine day for fishing," he said, and then turned to Jane. "I'm going to spend the whole day working on my book. It's not often I have the luxury of a whole day to myself! Could you fix a tray for me at dinner-time, Janie?"

"Of course, Papa," she replied cheerfully, and added: "It's lovely and peaceful, isn't it! I promise we won't bother you."

About fifteen minutes later, as she was washing the breakfast dishes, Papa stuck his head around the kitchen door.

"Jane, I hate to bother you, but I left my notebook up at the lighthouse last night. Could you get it for me, please? I'd send T. J., but I don't like him fooling around up there."

He took the great iron key from his pocket and handed it to her.

"No hurry, dear. Whenever it suits you."

A few minutes later as Jane fitted the key into the enormous lock of the lighthouse door, she felt a thrill of excitement. To have the whole lighthouse to herself!

It was cool, dim and very quiet in the little room at the base. The spiral staircase wound itself upward into shadow, and as Jane began to climb, the steps chimed, the echoes circling round and round inside the tower like wheeling birds.

When she reached the top a fierce brightness dazzled her eyes; pure, clear sun flooding in the glass windows and reflecting itself in the thousand sparkling eyes of the great cylinder.

Blinking, Jane opened the small door leading to the narrow catwalk that circled the top of the shaft. She stepped out. It was almost like stepping into space itself, into an enormous sea of windy blue.

Far below her the inlet rushed foaming from the bay to the ocean beyond, and the island lay before her, a living map. It stretched out, a long finger of sandy beach, with the surf curling at its edges like freshly washed lace. A ridge of blackly green cedars traced the center, delicate as a narrow bone. The roof of the big house below looked like a tiny wooden toy from a Christmas garden.

The wind, sweet and tangy with salt, sent Jane's long golden hair streaming. An inquisitive gull dipped to investigate, then banked and wheeled off toward the open sea. Jane circled to the seaward side of the catwalk to follow its flight. It was curious and fascinating to be looking down on a flying bird. She could trace the pearly gray back, the black edging of the wings and the sharp red slash of its beak.

It was just then that she saw the curl of smoke.

At first she thought that it was a strange little cloud floating near the surface of the water, or a vagrant fluff of morning fog. But then she could see a ship floating there, well out beyond the inlet breakers. The smoke was drifting upward above it.

Jane went back to the watch room and got the big telescope that was always kept on the shelf there. She returned to the catwalk. The telescope was heavy and she had some difficulty getting it open and positioned. By resting it on the railing of the catwalk and crouching down beside it she was able to focus its powerful eye.

Jane drew her breath in sharply. It was uncanny!

There, so close-seeming she felt herself to be a part of the scene, was the deck of a slender, elegant pleasure yacht. On the foredeck, in the bow, stood an enormously heavy lady wearing an elaborate hat perched atop her snowy hair. She was holding a little boy in a white sailor suit. Near her a young woman, also fashionably dressed, paced back and forth, wringing her hands.

A young, bearded man appeared to be shouting orders to two sailors. Jane could hear no sound, so it looked like a pantomime upon a stage. They had formed a fire line, and were dipping buckets on ropes overboard, passing them along, and throwing water on the cabin wall, where flame was licking upward in tiny tongues.

Just then a girl about Jane's age ran from behind the other side of the cabin. Her mouth was open in a silent scream. She began to climb the deck rail as if about to jump overboard. All about the burning ship the ocean lay calm and bright in the morning light.

Jane hurriedly replaced the telescope on the shelf. She ran as fast as she was able down the long, circular staircase.

Racing across the sandy yard that separated the lighthouse from the house, she burst breathless into the parlor. Papa was bent over his desk, writing busily.

"Oh, Papa!" she cried. "There's a ship burning— out beyond the inlet!"

Chapter Seventeen

Papa leaped to his feet, a worry line creasing his forehead. He listened quietly as Jane told him what she had just seen.

"Did you notice if she had any lifeboats?" Papa asked when Jane had finished.

"I didn't see any," she replied.

Papa frowned and shook his head.

"This could be very serious," he said. "All of our boats are gone—out after fish. In fact, all the men are gone. The weather's so fair we never expected any trouble today."

He rubbed the top of his head thinking.

"Where's T. J.?"

"In the kitchen," Jane replied. "He's fixing his crab traps."

"Well, you tell him to run as fast as he can down to Captain Cranmer's. I know the captain didn't go out for fish. His lumbago's been bothering him. But he'll have to help me, there's no one else."

"What can I do, Papa?" Jane caught the real worry in her father's voice.

"You go up to the widow's walk and signal with a sheet. At least they'll know we've seen them. Though how we'll get out in time, I don't know! We'll have to go clear down to Ship Bottom for a boat. What a time for this to happen! They could be in desperate trouble by then!"

Jane stood irresolutely. An idea had been stirring in her mind, but she still hesitated. She'd made a promise to William, and she didn't want to break it.

"What are you waiting for, child? Hurry!"

Jane bit her lip.

"Papa—I—I know where there's a boat."

Her father stared at her.

"But I know all the boats have gone out—" he began.

Jane grasped his sleeve and looked up into his face. She hated to break her word, but this was important.

"It's hidden, Papa. It's in the cedar grove, near the beach. It won't take nearly as long to get there as if you had to go 'way down to Ship Bottom."

And she told him exactly where to find the secret boat.

Papa didn't ask any questions. He simply accepted her word and hurriedly prepared to leave.

T. J. went dashing off on his errand.

As Papa went out the door he called back to Jane.

"Keep signaling. And be prepared to help care for the survivors. You and Mary will have to take full charge, for Mrs. Lippencott is sick today."

And he was gone, running down the road.

Jane snatched the big white tablecloth from the kitchen table and raced up to the top of the house to the widow's walk. Though the day was fair, a stiffish breeze was blowing and the cloth billowed out like a sail.

Above the ship smoke now curled black and ominous. Even without the spyglass, Jane could see fox-colored flames darting. She waved the tablecloth frantically, praying it would be seen. The ship was drifting helplessly on the quiet sea.

It seemed an eternity to Jane before she saw William's boat being pushed across the beach. It was so far down it looked like a toy, but by squinting she could see Papa and Captain Cranmer pushing, while T. J. ran ahead positioning the logs to roll her on.

It took so long to get the heavy boat down to the water that Jane was frantic with suspense. Finally however, its prow nosed into the surf. She saw Captain Cranmer take an oar, and Papa, wading and shoving, finally launched it and then leaped in. Luckily the sea was calm, and she saw them begin to pull at the oars in unison, heading out toward the burning ship.

About fifteen minutes later T. J. joined her on the widow's walk. He was soaked with sweat, and dropped exhausted to the floor.

"Boy," he wheezed, "am I tired!"

"Did Papa ask any questions about the boat?" Jane asked him.

"Nope. He was in too much of a hurry," T. J. replied, then added: "But you sure scotched William."

Jane nodded miserably.

"I know. I feel awful. He'll really be mad at me. But

honest, T. J.—I just didn't know what else to do! Those people might burn to death out there, or drown, if Papa had to go 'way down the island for a boat."

T. J. considered this silently.

"Yeah," he said finally, "I guess you had to. . . ."

The small rescue boat was making good time over the calm sea. They could see Papa and Captain Cranmer pulling with powerful even strokes. Jane now saw a white flag being waved from the bow of the burning ship.

"They've seen our signal," she cried.

T. J. scrambled to his feet to look.

"You stay here on watch," Jane told him, handing him the tablecloth. "I'm going down to get Mary, and we'll make some tea and soup."

It was well past noon with the sun high in a cloudless sky as Jane, Mary and T. J. stood on the beach watching the rescue boat make the end of its run through the breakers.

The boat seemed packed with people and was riding dangerously low in the water. The prevailing early afternoon wind had freshened, blowing from the southwest, and the surf was getting higher and rougher.

Jane suddenly had the strangest feeling.

A kind of cold terror gripped her. Her mind flashed back to that stormy day last March when she had stood helplessly on the beach as George Inman's body was carried ashore. It was a devastating feeling, this powerful sense of all this having happened before.

Jane gave an involuntary cry.

At almost the same moment Jane cried aloud, the fat lady stood up in the rescue boat. This sudden shift in weight rocked the overloaded boat. With a slow, almost gentle movement, it capsized.

Suddenly the surf was filled with shouting, flailing figures.

The little boy in the sailor suit had been flung from the fat lady's arms. He was caught up in a rolling wave. Without thinking, Jane waded into the churning water. Half swimming and splashing, her long skirt tangling about her legs, Jane made her way toward him and grasped his arm.

Another wave caught both of them off-balance. Jane felt herself being rolled and tumbled in its mighty thrust, her arm painfully scraping the sandy bottom. But she managed to cling to the little boy.

"You're all right," she choked, spitting salt water.

She grasped him tightly about the waist.

"You're safe now."

The child threw his arms about her neck in a death grip, nearly strangling her. Buffeted by the tumbling waves, Jane found the combined weight of the little boy and her own wet clothing almost more than she could manage. But finally, panting and stumbling, she floundered ashore.

Gently she tried to disengage the terrified child's arms, but he refused to let go, clinging to her in a kind of wild desperation. Jane staggered up the beach toward the wet and bedraggled group from the boat. Everyone had managed to get ashore safely. Even William's boat had washed in, and now lay upside-down on the beach.

Papa took charge quickly.

"We must get everyone up to the house," he said to Jane.

The fat lady approached her and took the little boy from her arms. She held him against her vast bosom, and patted his head. Grateful to be relieved of her burden, Jane ran with Mary up toward the big house.

For the next half hour Jane was kept busy trying to find dry clothing for everyone. She didn't take time to change her own wet things. An old dress of Mama's fitted the younger woman nicely, and Papa's extra shirts and trousers did for the bearded man and the two sailors. Jane's second-best calico went to the little girl, and one of T. J.'s suits, by rolling up the cuffs, fitted the little boy. But the fat lady was a real problem. She was enormous.

Jane scurried about in desperation. Finally, passing by William's room, Jane had an idea. His bed was covered with a huge turkey-red woven coverlet with long fringes. With scissors, Jane cut a slash in the center of it for a neck opening. Hesitantly she offered it to the older woman. The fat lady looked at it in astonishment and then began to laugh heartily.

Shortly thereafter she appeared in the kitchen, draped in the red coverlet, looking strange but regal as a pagan queen. She seemed to find it very amusing.

While the strangers from the ship were drying themselves and dressing in their borrowed clothes, Jane helped Mary to make fish chowder and a big pan of biscuits.

It was a curious assemblage that gathered about the big kitchen table. But they all appeared to be in good spirits, and hungrily attacked the hot and hearty dinner.

The bearded man had introduced himself as Mr. Clarence Courtenay. He told them how he and his family, wife, mother and two children, along with two sailors, had set sail on a pleasure cruise in their brand-new yacht. They were going from New York to Baltimore for her maiden run.

"I knew these waters were tricky" he said to Papa. "I haven't had much sailing experience, but I had good charts, and two men to help."

He was spooning up the chowder with relish.

"We hove to last night, just after dark," he went on. "I saw the Barnegat Lighthouse, and knew our location. But then I saw a small, moving light and thought it was another ship. So we came in nearer, thinking it was probably in safer water."

"There was a terrible bump," his wife broke in, "and we knew we'd run aground. I was terrified!"

"Our yacht was all right," Mr. Courtenay said. "We checked and there was no damage done, but we couldn't move. We were stuck on a sandy shoal. So we decided to wait until daylight to try to get help."

The fat lady reached for another biscuit.

"And then this morning that fool cooking-stove in the galley blew up," she said, shuddering. "I told Clarence that was a dangerous contraption."

T. J. was staring at her in awe. She was calmly buttering her sixth biscuit!

Mr. Courtenay looked at Papa.

"Words can never express our gratitude, sir," he said fervently.

Papa shook his head slowly.

"Mr. Courtenay," he said, "the truth of the matter is I feel we have been criminally negligent. This has been a bitter lesson to me."

He explained how the unexpected run of bluefish

had taken all the men and boats away from the island, and the fine weather had lulled his fears of any trouble occurring.

Papa looked over at Jane, who was sitting quietly. She was still damp and bedraggled. There was pride in his glance and in his voice was a great tenderness.

"If it hadn't been for my daughter," he said proudly, "you might all have been lost."

Jane felt a rush of blood warm her cheeks. Through a haze of fatigue she only half heard Papa tell of her sighting the ship from the top of the lighthouse, and of her knowledge of the only available lifeboat.

The rest of the day too passed in a kind of blur. Plans were made for Papa to take the Courtenays to Tuckerton tomorrow and make arrangements for their yacht to be pulled from the shoal and set afloat. The cabin quarters had been destroyed by the fire, and much repair was needed before she could sail again. Jane had to prepare supper for everyone later on and find sleeping accommodations for all of them.

Late that night as she snuggled into the bed she was temporarily sharing with T. J., she felt his small body suddenly begin to shake with laughter. Tired as she was, she raised up on one elbow.

"What's so funny?" she whispered.

"Wait till we tell William," he chortled softly. "I was just thinkin' about the fat lady in the red coverlet! William was goin' to use his boat to get a whale an' we really did bring in a whale with it, didn't we!"

He doubled up in a fresh paroxysm of glee.

Jane began to giggle. Their shared laughter swelled like a balloon, and finally they had to pull the quilt over their heads to muffle the sound.

-⊷ Chapter Eighteen ⊶-

It seemed strange to Jane to find herself completely
alone in the big house. The tick of the wag-on-the-wall
clock was the only sound, and an occasional snap from
the driftwood fire burning blue on the hearth. It sent
little shivers of flame streaming up in the strong
draft.

T. J. had gone with Papa in the skiff to take the
Courtenay family to Tuckerton, and Jane was all by
herself. Her sketch pad lay on her lap, but her drawing
was only begun, a few shadowy half-formed lines that
merely indicated the whelk case she was planning to
draw.

After the bustle of the past two days, she found that
she couldn't relax. Here she was, with all of this lovely
time to herself, with no one to find chores for her to
do, and she couldn't settle to anything.

It was almost with relief that Jane heard the knock on the front door. She was puzzled, for most people always came to the back of the house. She struggled with the heavy bolt and when she finally got it opened her astonishment deepened when she saw the old man who was standing there.

Jane had never really met Rob Speers, Dolly's grandfather. She knew him by sight, of course, but this was the first time she had ever spoken to him. Wind picked at the frayed edges of his worn coat and raggedy wisps of his white hair.

"Is your papa to home?" he asked, almost shyly.

"No," Jane replied, "I'm sorry, he's not here."

"Oh. Well, then—"

He turned to go, staggering slightly. He gripped the door jamb. Jane caught his hand to keep him from falling. It felt cold and frail.

"Do come in and rest for a moment," Jane urged, looking at him anxiously. He really did look quite ill and tired.

She helped him into the house and drew up a chair in front of the fire. The old man sat down diffidently.

"I didn't ought to be here—" he began.

Jane didn't quite know what to say to him.

"Papa's away just now," she explained, "and I'm the only one here. Could I fix you some tea, or something?"

He returned her smile and shook his head. Jane stiffened at the raw scent of whiskey that clung to him.

"No thankee, little missy. I'll be all right efen I kin jest set here for a spell. . . ."

He leaned forward and held out his hands to the fire.

"She ain't here, is she?" he mumbled, half to himself.

"Who?"

"The gurl—my Dolly—"

He raised his shaggy head and looked at her mutely. Something glistened in his rheumy old eyes, and Jane felt a sudden and terrible rush of pity for him. On impulse she knelt and took his cold hand in her own.

"Oh," she cried softly. "You don't know? Didn't she leave you any word at all? Have you been hunting for her?"

He nodded.

"A day an' a night now, it be," he said, "I been roamin' up an' down, lookin' an' callin'. Feared she might be drowned in the sea."

He clutched her hand. It was like a bird claw gripping her.

"Where'd she go? You know, little missy?"

Jane nodded.

"She—she went away," she answered him. "To—to get married."

"Married!" His eyes widened in surprise. "But—but—she's oney a little gurl!"

He suddenly dropped his face into his hands and rocked back and forth. Jane wanted to comfort him but she didn't know how.

"I know I weren't much good to her," he murmured brokenly, "but she were my kin. An' I do care for her. Such a merry, sassy little mite she were, jest like her ma."

Even in the midst of her pity Jane wanted to cry out. Oh, if you'd only told her that, just once! None of this would have happened! she thought angrily. Dolly thought you never cared about her.

But she held her tongue, for she couldn't bear to add to the old man's distress. Instead she patted his shoulder timidly.

"I'm sure she'll be all right," she lied with a valiant effort. "She'll be happy, I know."

He looked at her with a trace of suspicion.

"It weren't your brother she went with, were it?"

"William?" Jane stared at him in astonishment. "Oh, no, Mr. Speers! William's gone to college. Oh, you didn't think—?"

He sighed and shook his head.

"No, missy. Not really. I knowed she were terrible set on him, but he never paid her no mind. Who was the feller?"

"Well, his name is Frank," Jane replied hesitantly. "I don't really know him. They met at a dance at the hotel. . . ."

She felt suddenly ashamed.

"I—I begged her not to go," she said wretchedly.

For the first time, in a sudden flash, Jane realized that she herself was responsible in large part for what had happened. If I hadn't suggested running away in the first place Dolly might still be here, she thought miserably. But she couldn't bring herself to confess this to the old man.

Rob Speers stood up slowly, drawing his worn coat closer about his stooped shoulders.

"Well, what's done's done," he said, heading for the door. "Efen Dolly sends you any word of her whereabouts, you'll let me know?"

His question was almost tentative.

"Oh, yes—yes, I surely will," Jane promised fervently. "As soon as I hear, I'll let you know."

After the old man had gone, Jane returned to the parlor and sat down in front of the fire.

How do things get so twisted up? she thought. People feeling one thing, and doing another. It's all so crazy!

She thought about the old man, wandering the beach at night with his lantern, searching for the granddaughter he'd never seemed to care anything about.

The moving lantern in the night!

Jane sat up suddenly.

She remembered Mr. Courtenay's words, "—and then we saw a moving light and thought it was another ship. . . ."

Inadvertently, old Rob Speers had lured the yacht onto the shoal!

What a strange and mystifying series of events! Like the links of a chain, one small thing leading to another, and another and another!

Because of me! Jane thought.

Because of me, in a moment of anger, wanting to run away, Dolly was gone, a ship was wrecked, William's secret was revealed.

Jane drew her breath in sharply. It seemed as if every event led into the next in a kind of frightening progression; that without even realizing it, your smallest act could affect people you didn't even know!

Jane's mind was still whirling around several hours later when Papa and T. J. returned.

Papa gave her a giant bear hug, and thrust a package into her hand.

"Here's a little present for our heroine!" he laughed.

Jane blushed and held back. She felt like anything but a heroine!

"Go ahead. Open it," T. J. urged.

It was a big paper sack full of striped molasses-mint humbugs, which Jane adored, and a packet of six brand-new drawing pencils.

"I couldn't get a sketchbook," Papa said. "The shops in Tuckerton don't have such refinements. But we do have some good news! There was a wire at the telegraph office. Mama will be coming home next Saturday!"

Jane stuffed a humbug into her mouth to hide her disappointment. She mumbled something she hoped was appropriate, and turned away to put dinner on the table.

"I think it's done Mama good to get away from the island for awhile," Papa said cheerfully. "It gets pretty bleak for a woman out here. But she misses all of us."

-⋙Chapter Nineteen⋘-

As Jane dressed on Saturday morning, she made a decision. During what Papa called "a white night," Jane had done a lot of thinking. She could not bring herself to forgive Mama for forbidding her friendship with Dolly. She felt this had been cruel, and had really been the cause of all the trouble.

But Jane also knew now that running away from home was not the answer to her problems with Mama. She loved Papa and William and T. J. too much to do that. She knew that she belonged with them, that she was part of a family and was needed.

But Mama didn't need her. And Jane didn't need Mama. So—they'd just have to live with that!

Jane had decided she didn't want to be at home when Mama arrived. That way I won't have to pretend I'm happy, she thought, and at least she can't accuse me of lying!

She had decided to spend the day at her rock cave on the shore. The rocks were covered with ancient barnacles that looked like tiny white stone-roses, and Jane had been wanting to make a drawing of them. Mama would be home and settled in by suppertime, and then Jane could just walk in casually, with no particular pretense of joy.

Jane fixed a good hot breakfast for Papa and T. J. and afterward she set the kitchen in order. She fixed a lunch for herself of bread and cheese and apples, which she put into a string bag along with her sketch pad and her new drawing pencils.

Without telling anyone where she was going, Jane slipped out of the house about midmorning and made her way across the dunes to the beach.

It was the kind of autumn day she loved best. Great blindingly white cloud galleons sailed majestically over the sea, and the blue water sparkled with a thousand dancing sun glints.

The tide was ebbing, and tiny sandpipers raced before the incoming waves like small whispers of shadow across the wet sand. The gulls and terns stood in dignity among the smaller birds, feeding on surf clams washed up by the tide. It was a white and blue world of movement and sound, vast and open and free, and Jane felt its beauty flood over her, leaving her as light and clean as the windy beach.

She clambered over the first large rock and was making her way across its sloping surface when suddenly the handle of the old string bag broke. The bag containing her drawing things and her lunch went plunging down into a crevice between the rocks.

"Oh, darn it!" Jane exclaimed in disgust.

The crevice was fairly wide, and Jane could see the contents of the bag spilled over the sand below. She could replace the lunch, but not the drawing things. It was her last sketch pad. It was only about eight or ten feet down, but too far to reach even by hanging over the edge of the rock.

Jane studied the situation for a moment. Then she decided to try to get down to it by lowering herself carefully, pressing her back against one side of the rock and her feet against the opposite one.

Cautiously she positioned herself and began to inch her way down slowly. In such cramped quarters she couldn't move very fast, but bit by bit she was making progress.

Then suddenly it happened!

The worn soles of her old shoes were slippery. Her foot touched a smooth place on the rock's side. There was a fierce, blinding flash of pain in her head, and blackness flooded over her.

When Jane finally opened her eyes it was to a world whirling with golden sparks. At first she couldn't focus her eyes properly. It seemed to her that she was at the center of a great fire, with little orange flames fizzing all about her. Her head ached unmercifully.

Gradually, however, her vision cleared a bit. She realized that she was lying on the sand at the bottom of the crevice. Above her she could see a slice of blue sky.

She moved to sit up, and her vision swam once again. It made her feel dizzy and sick and it was only by clutching her hands tightly together and digging her nails into her palms that she kept from throwing up.

She lay quietly for a few moments. It seemed to her that something was strangely wrong. There wasn't much room in the small space between the rocks where she had fallen, but she certainly was lying in a peculiar position. Her left leg didn't seem to be in the proper place.

Gingerly, moving an inch at a time, Jane pulled herself into a partly upright position. Her long skirt had been twisted up in the fall, and she could see a creeping stain of blood on her long underdrawers. Absurdly, she remembered something T. J. had once said when he got a fishhook caught in his hand: "I certainly do hate the sight of blood—especially my own!"

Cautiously, for even the slightest movement made her head swim, Jane leaned over. A bit at a time she pulled up the bloodstained linen. Between her knee and her ankle she could see the shattered end of her leg bone protruding, with blood seeping slowly around it.

Jane uttered a small, strangled cry.

Darkness once again enveloped her.

When her senses finally returned—Jane would never know how much time had elapsed—she lay very still. She tried to fight her rising panic.

She knew that she was trapped. She could never climb out of the crevice by herself. Her only hope lay in the chance of someone finding her.

Gathering all of her strength, Jane began to call. "Help! Help! Papa—T. J.—"

The wind caught her voice and sent it bouncing back and forth against the rock walls. It sounded like the faint mewing of a kitten.

"Help me. . . . Oh, help me. . . ."

She was too far away from the house to be heard.

Finally, exhausted by even this small effort, a kind of lethargy seemed to engulf her. She felt numb. Occasionally a sea gull winged across her patch of sky, and she noticed dully that the great white clouds were massing and growing darker. She began to feel cold.

Some desperate instinct told her that she must try to move to keep herself warm. And she knew if she were going to move she would have to do something about her leg.

Curiously, she did not feel much pain from the broken leg. It was the bump on her head that was throbbing incessantly. With a tremendous effort Jane began to rip the ruffle from the bottom of her white linen petticoat. It seemed to take forever, but finally she managed to tear it loose. It would serve as a bandage for her injured leg.

Keeping her eyes averted so she couldn't see the blood, she started at the ankle and wound the makeshift bandage as tightly as she could stand it around and around, feeling with her fingers.

It seemed to take hours to accomplish. When she was finished she was covered with sweat and panting with exhaustion.

She pulled herself to a sitting position with great effort and lifted her leg with her hands, extending it flat on the sand.

Surely someone would miss her soon. She had no

idea what time it was, but surely someone would come hunting for her. And then she remembered with dismay—no one knew about the rock cave but Dolly!

The clouds were darkening rapidly now, and a wind from the sea moaned through the crevice. Jane pulled her long skirt up over her shoulders, huddling down into it for warmth. A first drop of rain spatted against the rock and bounced off.

Jane closed her eyes against the pain that surged up in her head, and once again darkness stole over her mind like a great soft wing.

-◄ Chapter Twenty ►-

Jane opened her eyes slowly. She was conscious of a feeling of delicious warmth and softness. A tender, diffused golden light seemed to wrap her in a filmy gauze.

She turned her head slightly and discovered to her slow surprise that she was in her own bed. The light came from a kerosene lamp on the table. It was quiet and night shadow filled the corners of the room.

Jane felt rather than heard a faint creak from the rocking chair, and a whisper of a rustle.

Mama was bending over her.

"Hello, Mama."

Suddenly Mama's face was pressed against hers on the pillow. She was held close in a loving embrace.

"Oh, Jane—Janie, darling. . . ."

Mama's face was wet with tears.

She spoke no more, only held Jane close. It was so peaceful and good that Jane drifted off to sleep again.

When she awoke the next time sun was splashing itself in great bright pools on the floor of her room. Papa, Mama and Dr. DiGiovanni were standing at the foot of her bed.

In her surprise at seeing them Jane tried to sit up. She was amazed to find that she couldn't quite manage it. She was weak as a cat, and the lower part of her body felt as if it was made of wood.

"Aha!" cried Dr. DiGiovanni, clapping his hands together. "Our leetle sleeping beauty—she awakes!"

Mama took Jane's hand in her own.

"How are you feeling, dear?"

Jane noticed that there were wells of shadow under Mama's eyes, and her face looked wan and tired.

"Oh, I'm just fine," she answered cheerfully. "What happened?"

Then a sudden swift memory flashed through her mind.

"Oooh—my leg!"

Involuntarily she reached down. Her left leg was encased in enormous, heavy bandages. It felt like a lump of lead.

"Ah, good!" the doctor exclaimed. "She remembers!"

He bent down and laid a hand on her forehead.

"Da fever, she ees gone. Now I theenk our leetle Zhanie weel be well again!"

He waggled his finger at her.

"Thees one ees a tough one," he said.

Jane was looking at her parents and the doctor in

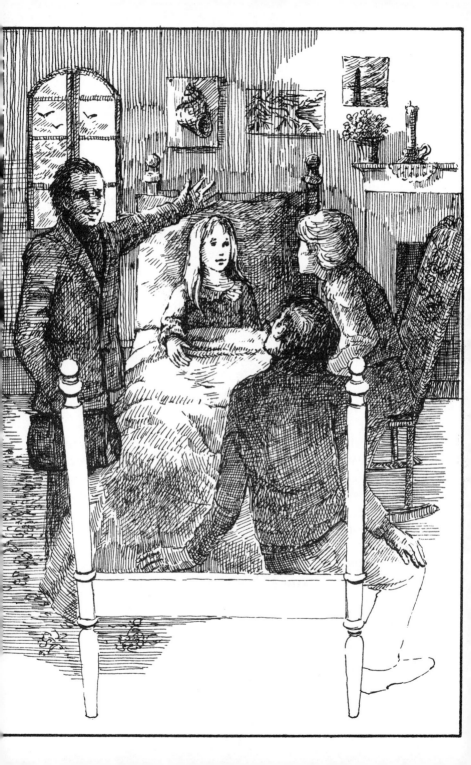

bewilderment. She was trying to remember, but only snatches and fragments of things danced through her mind—the rocks, the pain and the terror. . . .

A soft sob escaped her.

"Oh! Now I remember! I fell, and I thought no one would ever find me."

Papa sat down gently on the bed beside her.

"You've had a narrow squeak, Janie," he said. "No one knew where you were. We didn't really begin to worry until dinnertime came."

The whole accident now flashed in front of Jane.

"We searched and searched, all of us," Papa continued, "and finally Mama thought of the rocks. You were lying there, unconscious."

The doctor smiled.

"Zhanie, you mees da great rescue operation!"

Even Papa could smile now, though his face too was tired and pale.

"It was T. J. who helped," he said to Jane. "The crevice was too narrow for me to get down. So we lowered T. J. on a rope, and he tied the rope around you and we hauled you up like a little sack of flour. He was a brave little lad! He was so frightened when you didn't speak to him—he thought you were dead."

Jane couldn't speak for a moment.

"I don't remember anything about that," she said at last.

Mama was smoothing her pillow.

"No, dear. You had a concussion. You must have struck your head on the rock when you fell."

Jane nodded.

"I remember I had an awful headache."

The doctor was shaking his head slowly.

"I tell you all. Thees leetle Zhanie, she is someting! To put a bandage on her own leg! That ees—how you say it?—great courage!"

Jane looked anxiously at the doctor.

"My leg—will it be all right?"

"Ah, but certainly!" He nodded vigorously. "Mind you, that was a bad break—eet was what we call a compound fracture. But yes, yes, in time eet will heal and be well."

Just then a small, tousled head poked around the door.

"Hey, Jane!"

T. J. came bounding into the room.

She smiled at him wanly.

"Sure glad you're all right now," he said, coming up to the bed. "You was outa your head for five days, an' we thought you was goin' to die!"

"Hush!" Mama cautioned him sharply.

Jane couldn't believe it.

"Five days!" she exclaimed weakly.

Mama glanced at the doctor, who nodded.

"Yes, dear, you've been very ill," she explained quietly. "Concussion and shock, with a bad fracture. You were delirious with a fever. That's what T. J. meant."

Mama turned to the others.

"Now, all of you—out of here! Jane needs to rest."

Papa squeezed Jane's hand.

"Sleep now, Janie. We'll see you later."

When everyone had gone, Mama held Jane's head up and gave her something warm and fragrant to drink. Jane smiled at her mother.

"I'm glad you're home, Mama," she said softly.

--⊷{ Chapter Twenty-One }⊶--

Papa closed the magazine and leaned back in the rocking chair, still laughing.

"I do like this Mark Twain fellow," he said, still chuckling.

He had just finished reading aloud to Jane a new story called "The Celebrated Jumping Frog of Calaveras County."

"Oh, Papa," she giggled. "That *was* good!"

Rain was clicking against the window, but Jane's room was cozy and bright. A merry little fire snapped in the Franklin stove, casting a rosy light on all her beloved possessions.

On the table beside her bed sat two apple dolls Mary had given her. Mary came to visit her every day, and they'd built a miniature room from an old wooden box, making the tiny furnishings together.

Jane gave a soft sigh of satisfaction.

"Oh, I really do love this room," she said.

Papa smiled.

"Well, now, that's rather a good thing. You've spent five weeks cooped up in here—and you still love it?"

Jane nodded contentedly.

"I love this room, and this house, and the island and—all of you! Everyone has been so good to me!"

She paused. There was something she had been wanting to say for a long time.

"Papa, there's something I've been wanting to tell you. I don't quite know how, for it's not very nice. . . . But I've just got to say it—"

She hesitated, and then plunged ahead.

"The day of my accident I—I went down to the rocks because I didn't want to see Mama. I was angry at her, about Dolly, and a lot of other things, and I—oh, Papa, before that I'd been planning to run away."

The whole sorry story came pouring out in a rush.

Papa listened quietly, his face grave and attentive. When Jane had finished he sat down on the bed beside her.

"I'm glad you told me, Janie. It's a good thing to clear the air."

"Papa—I'm so ashamed!"

Papa studied her for a moment.

"I'm going to tell you something, Jane. I think that now you're old enough to understand. You know, I think that sometimes I forget what it really means for a family to live in the shadow of a lighthouse. It puts a great responsibility on everyone, even the children.

You have to learn to take care of others, and it's not easy. For me it's been a good life. I've regained my health, and learned many things, but—"

He hesitated, looking earnestly at Jane.

"I know that it often seems to you that Mama is very strict and demanding. It's true, she was very upset about you and Dolly. She felt that Dolly wasn't the right sort of friend for you. Mama knew that you were sneaking off to the rocks to meet her secretly."

A hot flush of blood crimsoned Jane's cheeks.

"You mean—she knew all the time!"

"Yes. And she felt that she—well, that she couldn't reach you anymore. She was so distressed about it that finally I thought it would be a good idea if she got away for awhile, for a little visit with her parents."

"Oh, Papa—I didn't know."

"Jane, I want to explain to you something about Mama. She loves you so much that she wants you to be—well, perfect, I guess. This isn't fair to you, I know. But sometimes when people love a great deal they get a little . . . shortsighted. Mama wants you to be just like she is, and you—well, be truthful—you want Mama to think the same way you do."

Papa looked at her intently.

"Am I making any sense to you?"

Jane nodded.

"Yes. I think I understand, honest I do."

He got up and began to pace the floor, his hands thrust deep in his pockets.

"You see," he said, "when I took sick and we had to come to the island, Mama was very unhappy. She loves the city—she loves to go shopping, and to parties. She was always used to a fine house, and pretty clothes and lots of friends.

"She's lonely here, and a little frightened too. It's a rough sort of life for a woman, with the wind and the hard work, and the loneliness, especially for a gentlewoman like Mama."

For the first time Jane was beginning to see her mother in a new light.

"Mama's been so gallant. She feels such a great responsibility for you and William and T. J. She wants you to grow up properly, to be able to take your places in the world. And she found it hard to understand that all of you have discovered great beauty and value here, in this simple life."

Papa pointed to Jane's drawings pinned to the wall.

"Mama wasn't able to understand that you're trying to express what you've found here on the island. To her, these were just a frivolous pastime, something you were doing when you should have been learning to cook and sew and do all the things a lady should know how to do. But I think that now she is beginning to realize what you are, the kind of person you are."

Papa crossed the room and took Jane's face in his hands.

"Janie," he said softly, "I think you've done a lot of growing up this year—I think we all have."

He kissed her forehead.

"Now you must get some rest. Don't forget, tomorrow is the big day—you try out your crutches for the first time!"

Some time later there was a tap at her door. Jane

rubbed her eyes dazedly. She must have fallen asleep.

Mama came in with her supper tray. She plumped Jane's pillow and set the tray on the bed beside her.

"There's a letter for you," she announced.

On the tray was a small envelope. Jane picked it up, surprised. She didn't often get a letter.

She opened it hastily and began to read.

> Dear Jane
> i wanted to rite and tell you im fine i hope you are to. i got a good job with som nice folks i got a new green dress with my own mony i earned. i can ride the horse cars on my haf day you wood lik this place its fun.
>
> love,
> DOLLY

When she had finished reading, Jane looked guiltily at her mother.

"It's from—Dolly," she said, hesitating.

"Yes, I thought it might be," Mama said. "Is she well?"

"Yes—she says . . . well, here, you can read it." Jane handed her the letter.

"No, thank you. It's your letter." Mama bent and brushed an invisible speck from her skirt.

Jane studied the return address.

"She's in Philadelphia," she said.

"Yes," Mama replied, "she's staying with the Grants."

Jane looked at her mother in surprise.

"How did you know that, Mama?"

Mama's face colored brightly. She seemed a bit flustered.

"Well . . . you were so ill that I didn't have the opportunity to tell you." Her mother's voice sounded unusually brisk. "The day I left for Philadelphia, I saw Dolly at the stage stop in Tuckerton. She was crying and in a terrible state. She didn't make much sense at all, but I gathered that she was going to run off with some boy, and that he'd left her there."

Mama got up and began to poke at the fire, her back to Jane.

"Well, I couldn't just leave the child there," she said sharply, almost as if in apology.

Jane began to smile.

"Hmmm. Well, I bought her a ticket and took her with me. The Grants needed a hired girl, and Mrs. Grant is a very motherly woman. That child needs a mother to look after her. . . ."

Mama's words trailed off.

"Oh, Mama!" Jane cried softly, "I'm so glad! That was very kind of you."

Mama certainly was full of surprises! To hide her emotion, Jane took a bite of chicken. Then a thought struck her.

"Mama, we must tell Dolly's grandfather. He was so worried."

"He already knows," Mama said crisply. "I stopped by his house the day I returned from Philadelphia."

She shook her head, speaking almost to herself. "No wonder the girl wanted to run away. I must see to it that something is done about that pathetic old man, and those boys. . . ."

At the doorway she turned and said, "Mind you, Jane Sibylla—you eat all of that chicken. You need it for strength."

Jane grinned, and picked up a chicken wing.

PART FOUR

December
1870

-*≪ Chapter Twenty-Two ≫*-

"This is absolutely the last bunch of greens I'm car-ryin' in here," T. J. warned Jane as he dumped an armload of glossy-green laurel beside her chair.

He flung himself flat on the parlor floor.

"Such a darn lot of fuss for a dumb old weddin'," he complained. "Mama's drivin' me near crazy with er-rands! It's facetious, that's what it is—just plain, down-right facetious!"

"Facetious?" Jane raised an eyebrow. "Whatever happened to anachronistic?"

T. J. got to his feet with dignity.

"It's a new word. And if you're so dumb you can just go look it up in Papa's dictionary. I'm goin' down to the dock to wait for William."

He thrust his hands in his pockets and stalked out of the room.

Jane could hear Mama's voice.

"T. J.—I need some more butternuts cracked. You just come along to the kitchen now. Don't dawdle so."

A spicy scent of mincemeat drifted across the hall.

Jane, leaning on her crutch, looked around the parlor with satisfaction. Tomorrow would be Christmas Day, and Mary and Dr. DiGiovanni were to be married right here in this room. Jane was to be the bridesmaid, probably the only bridesmaid in the world on crutches, she thought, but she did have a beautiful new dress of shell-pink silk to wear.

Laurel chains garlanded the doors and mantel and fresh pine banked the windowsills. The Christmas tree stood tall and proud in a red wooden tub, heavy with popcorn and cranberry chains and tiny frosted gingerbread stars.

In a corner of the room, draped with a sheet behind the old Chinese screen, was Jane's own special secret surprise gift to the family, to be unveiled tonight.

Just then Mama stuck her head in the doorway.

"The boat's in," she announced. "William's here."

Jane hobbled after her across the hall and into the kitchen. They opened the door and stood together in a swash of lamplight spilling out across the yard. Mama's hand rested lightly on Jane's shoulder. They saw lanterns bobbing, and heard voices shouting, and Papa and William came into view, their arms laden with packages. Jane breathed deep of the cold salt air, an unutterable happiness welling in her.

Supper that night was a festive affair, with everyone talking at once. They had their traditional oyster stew, and sticky buns dark with cinnamon and raisins.

Mama brought a pumpkin pie to the table, still warm from the oven.

"Guess what?" she laughed. "One of my Christmas gifts to the whole family is . . . the prunes are all gone!"

A general cheer went up around the table.

Later they all gathered about the Christmas tree. It was a moment of breathtaking solemnity as Papa took a long paper spill from the holder and lit it at the hearth fire. As he touched the glowing end to each tiny candle, the tree slowly took shape until finally it stood shimmering from top to bottom. T. J. clapped his hands in delight.

"Facetious!" he exclaimed.

Laughter broke the spell of wonder and silence.

As the candles burned down, they exchanged their gifts. Mama loved the heart-shaped beaded pincushion Jane had made for her, and Papa was glowing over a copy of Melville's *Moby Dick* William had found for him. T. J.'s gift was a new pair of ice skates, shining steel runners to strap to his boots, and Mary's present was a bright new shawl, and for baby Georgie a stocking dolly Mama had made. Jane hugged her new sketchbook and a box of watercolor paints. William was quite overwhelmed with his gift—a new pocket watch.

At last Jane lifted herself out of her chair and stood leaning lightly on her crutch.

"All right now," she announced. "Everyone must sit down, so you can see it properly."

T. J. helped her, and together they folded back the old Chinese screen.

Jane's secret surprise gift was revealed.

On the table stood a round, chip-wood basket, filled with sand and garlanded with ribbon. In it stood a graceful tree branch, polished silver-smooth by salt and wind, about four feet high. It was hung with all manner of treasures from the beach.

At the top stood a huge starfish, and creamy whelk cases, like flower garlands, curved from branch to branch. Soft lilac and brown moon shells swung their spirals, and rosy conchs swirled slowly on threads. On great, flat clam shells Jane had glued tiny jingle shells, smoked-pearl and orange-gold, and ferny bits of seaweed, and these too swung gently, glinting in the firelight. Bits of beach glass, ruby and cobalt and emerald, winked like little eyes, and elongated oyster shells shone on the silvery branches like huge raindrops.

"It's a sea tree!" Jane said.

There was a long moment of silence as everyone looked in wonder at the exquisite little tree.

Papa leaped to his feet.

"Janie! It's the most beautiful tree in the world!"

Everyone crowded around to examine it more closely and admire it. Even Mama was impressed.

"What a lovely thing!" she cried, and then added: "It's certainly—unusual!"

Then she glanced at the clock.

"Good heavens! Look at the time!" she cried. "Papa has second watch, and in case you've forgotten—we have a wedding here tomorrow!"

Laughing, they all gathered up their gifts and extinguished the candles on the Christmas tree. Papa pulled on his heavy coat and headed for the lighthouse to relieve Mr. Lippencott.

Jane and William stood together in the kitchen doorway, watching his lantern bob across the yard. Above the house, serene across the cold starry sky, the pure, clear beam of the great light swept its giant arc.

"William," Jane said, "I'm sorry about your boat —about having to tell, I mean."

William put his hand on her shoulder.

"That's all right," he said quietly. "You did the right thing, Jane."

"You know," Jane said, "Papa said something once. He said that when you live in the shadow of a lighthouse you just have to take more responsibility than most folks. I guess he meant that other people have to come first, before yourself."

"Well," William replied cheerfully, "that's not such a bad thing, is it?"

Just then Mama's crisp voice interrupted them.

"Come now, the two of you! You'll catch your death, standing there in the cold! Hurry now, and get to bed. Tomorrow's going to be a very busy day and I'm counting on both of you."

Jane looked up at William and they both began to laugh.

"See what I mean?" she said.

ABOUT THE AUTHOR

Marden Dahlstedt lives on Long Beach Island, where *Shadow of the Lighthouse* is set. She is librarian at the Beach Haven Elementary School, and in summer, she and her husband run an antique store, the Attic.

Shadow of the Lighthouse is Marden Dahlstedt's second book. Her first book, *The Terrible Wave,* is about a girl's experiences during the 1889 Johnstown Flood. She grew up hearing stories of the flood from her grandparents, who were living in Johnstown when it occurred.

Mrs. Dahlstedt was born and grew up in Pittsburgh, Pennsylvania. She received her BA from Chatham College and her librarian certification from Slippery Rock State College. She and her husband have lived for five years on the island, four miles off the coast of New Jersey.

ABOUT THE ARTIST

Judith Gwyn Brown was born and grew up in New York City, where she presently makes her home. She studied art history at New York University before beginning her career as an illustrator. She has illustrated more than thirty books, including *Muffin,* which she also wrote, *Mandy, Daisy,* and *The Best Christmas Pageant Ever.*